Valley of the Dogs

Dark Stories

By

James Musgrave

EMRE Publishing Fiction

San Diego, CA

ISBN: 978-1-943457-47-2

Published by EMRE Publishing Fiction
San Diego, CA

Valley of the Dogs
Dark Stories

By

James Musgrave

© 2021 by James Musgrave

Published by English Majors, Reviewers and Editors, LLC

An English Majors, Reviewers and Editors Book Copyright 2021
Cover Illustration by A. R. Mirabal, neotino.net

English Majors, Reviewers and Editors Publishers is a publishing house based in San Diego, California.

Website: emrepublishing.com

For more information, please contact:

English Majors, Reviewers and Editors, LLC

Other Works by This Author

Forevermore: A Pat O'Malley Historical Mystery

Disappearance at Mount Sinai: A Pat O'Malley Historical Mystery

Jane the Grabber: A Pat O'Malley Steampunk Mystery

Steam City Pirates: A Pat O'Malley Steampunk Mystery

The Digital Scribe: A Writer's Guide to Electronic Media

Lucifer's Wedding

Sins of Darkness

Russian Wolves

Iron Maiden an Alternate History

Love Zombies of San Diego

Freak Story: 1967-1969

The President's Parasite and Other Stories

The Mayan Magician and Other Stories

Catalina Ghost Stories

Chinawoman's Chance

The Spiritualist Murders

The Stockton Insane Asylum Murder

The Angel's Trumpet

Dark Justice

The Dancing Murders

For all my grandchildren and great-grandchildren. You know who you are. Thank God, because I can't keep up with you!

Interactive and Multimedia Enhanced eBooks

EMRE Publishing is now selling completely "enhanced" versions of its books through the unique Embellisher Multimedia Stream platform. Simply register inside the eReader to have access to the variety of titles. They contain relevant historical videos, music, interactive content, and a complete audiobook edition in many of the great titles.

Visit https://emrepublishing.com/new_embellisher-ereader/ to see what's available. Enter your email and a password to register and view. Buy your future digital copies of this Portia of the Pacific Historical Mystery series at reduced prices here: https://books.bookfunnel.com/portiaofpacific

"If you only read the books that everyone else is reading, you can only think what everyone else is thinking."— Haruki Murakami, *Norwegian Wood*

Preface

Entering the consciousness of a reader is the most sacred enterprise an author can have. These stories have been collected as my Zen reflection during the past year's COVID-19 plague. This shamanistic mental state, which the Japanese term "Mushin," or "no-mind" is close to the stream-of-consciousness technique that Henry James, Virginia Woolf, Jack Kerouac, James Joyce, and William Faulkner used to such success. However, it is also a form of channeling that defies definition. This is the mystical realm that creatives around the world know so well, and we worship at its altar every day we put fingers to keys or pen to paper. I want to thank readers who enjoy dark stories, as in this age of political correctness and what publishers often term "accessibility," it is becoming more difficult for us authors, especially us authors who don't make a lot of money from our work, to find an audience. I will go out on a limb and say that if the author does make a lot of money from a dark story, he/she will get marketing to back him/her up to ride the tide of money to the bank. If you ride this wave of Gustav and all the other characters in my collection, then thanks for that. It's been a tough year for all of us. Bless you.

Award-winning short fiction author, Jacob M. Appel says, "With the publication of *Valley of the Dogs*, Jim Musgrave joins the ranks of George Saunders, Steven Millhauser, and Kevin Brockmeier at the heart of the modern American short story's second great renaissance."

Introduction

Hollywood and Broadway are icons of the American Dream. But what happens to those who feed off that dream? Just as drug cartels have many underlings, who must get paid along the journey to the addicts, so do the characters who need to be nourished by the luminaries who make up this star-studded world above us. James Musgrave's collection of eleven stories, in many ways, addresses the theme of "star power," but in a way that satirizes the stereotypical "Hollywood endings" in very unique and literary ways. This collection has a remedy for the past year's traumas caused by a worldwide pandemic.

The first story, "Another Metamorphosis Rag," kicks off the eleven-story set very well. Franz Kafka, during a visit to New York City from Prague, gets almost forced into a lyric-writing gig to replace one of the famed Broadway musical brothers, Ira Gershwin, in the early 1920s. What happens is both humorous and tragic, as Kafka would want it to be, like Kafka and his Prague group of fellow authors used to laugh uproariously during Franz's reading of such supposedly serious novels as *The Trial*. Musgrave's little piece also makes light of and forces us to look more seriously at, what his fate may have been on Broadway.

The second story "The Annulment" is another Kafka family story. This time, it concerns Franz's little sister, Ottla, who was his favorite. I will not ruin this one for you, except to say that it is based on fact, and it takes a Kafkaesque turn for the worse, and yet remains true to the dark and surreal form of all Kafka stories. Truly, it is a tale for any pandemic, political or otherwise.

"Communion" takes place in the author's place of birth, Fall River, Massachusetts. He told me that his aunt had been committed to a mental institution under similar circumstances, but his plot is completely fictional. However, as I read it, I keep picturing all the people forced into many kinds of isolation during the past year, and it suddenly became a very prescient and very scary tale indeed. The ending is one I pondered for quite some time to see how the plot's logic was a tragedy within a tragedy.

"Jasmine" is my favorite story. Why? Because it reflects both the predicament of those elders who faced the most hardships during the past year, and it is also a very dark love story of spiritual belief beyond the Judeo-Christian ethos. I will let you see what this ending does for you to make your conclusions. Again, Musgrave has woven a story within a story, both of these stories rather tragically rendered but effective.

The tale "I'm Goin' Down" strikes at the heart of suicidal ideation for so many veterans and their families. Mr. Musgrave's father was a Pearl Harbor Survivor and a hero, who worked for the military in a civilian capacity for thirty years. Musgrave himself is a Vietnam Era Vet. He told me he crafted this story after hearing the Billie Eilish song "Listen Before I Go." He realized that the younger generation who are related to vets are also affected by their parent's suicide, and so, after researching a bit, he wrote this story to address the problem of recognition in an interestingly literary way. He told me that vets and kids of vets also get categorized as not being literary, so he also wanted to show opposition to that stereotype.

"The Jain" introduced me to a new religion. Unlike the author, I have never studied Vedanta or Buddhism, and certainly not Jainism. However, the stark juxtaposition this story makes between military values and religious values causes one to think very deeply about how similar we are around the world in our extreme ways of perceiving so-called "reality." A family can be a microcosmic truth for you, if you are not fully aware or "awake," as the Buddhists call it. When you do become awake, however, it can cause the problems you can see in this story. It is certainly not a Western "thank you for your service" kind of story, but it does damage your eyes as a reader.

"The Prophet" fits the dark theme of this collection, as well as its satirical reflection on social media fame, like that of Billie Eilish. The beginning quote by Meister Eckhardt shows a version of God that goes beyond the "ceramic universe" reflected in the Bible. Musgrave, I happen to know, is a vegetarian and a Vedanta follower. In this belief system, God takes on a much larger and more personal role in the human psyche, and the danger comes about when the initiate is "star-struck" by His powers and mistakenly believes he or she can speak for Him. In this story, the spokesperson is a refugee from Central America during the lockdown, wherein the gangs have become much more active and dangerous. After a traumatic rape, the main character escapes to San Diego, where she becomes an online spiritual teen celebrity, of sorts. When the female psychiatrist is called upon to assist, however, the doctor is the person who learns what the power of God can really do.

Musgrave informed me he included this second Lady Gaga-inspired story, "The Church of Lady Haha," because it features drugs that have been recently seen as quite effective in the treatment of PTSD and other psychoses. He said a literary magazine had an internal brouhaha about publishing it, as this was before the recent research came out about peyote. Since it never was published, he decided to include it in this volume, and I'm so glad he did. The setting and the characters are so originally crafted that one wonders if they aren't running their business somewhere right now. If not, then there's probably a version of their care-giving coming down the line fairly soon.

Similar to "The Prophet," the story "The Visionary" is based on a refugee who makes a long journey up into the United States to flee gang harassment of the main character's family, and he does something about it. However, it happens after telling the reader a lot about why his mother said he was a genius child. As many minority groups within a culture, the Ladinos are often persecuted, but when you're also indigenous, the problems are doubled. Musgrave's ending may not be the most pleasant, but it's a fact that many refugees have faced even worse choices, so the resolution works for this reader.

The story, "Asterisk," is a futuristic and modern science fiction tale. The English professor character in the story is faced with allowing students who have been surgically implanted with an advanced computer into his course. Liberal Arts and Literature classes are quickly disappearing, and this causes both classroom instruction and sociological problems that go well beyond the inside of the classroom. This tale is dark, as well, and the ending makes you believe we may be heading in this direction. Read books about the new hierarchy of the "Meritocracy," which has replaced the old "Aristocracy" of the previous generations, and has caused a rich/poor gap much wider than during the Victorian Era. What might we call this? Perhaps the "Androidocracy"? At any rate, this professor attempts to make a final stand against its rapid advance.

The title story, "Valley of the Dogs," is a yarn told from the viewpoint of one of legendary songstress Lady Gaga's three French bulldogs. His name is Gustav. Gustav can talk. Just as we have had to do during the last year's game of Zoom, Gustav also has to communicate with us in an act of sheer desperation. This story happened (read the news), so Gustav has something to say, and, at the crucially climactic moment, he says it. His message is one we should all understand—humanoids, animals, and villains.

I hope you enjoy these eleven stories as much as I did. As an American Studies Professor for over twenty-five years, I can't say that I've ever read a short work that so startlingly demonstrates human frailty, love, and hatred in such stark terms. Mr. Musgrave's mind is certainly one to rival any of the modern storytellers we have today.

Matteo Lesser, Ph.D., retired Professor of American Studies, San Diego, CA.

Table of Contents

Another Metamorphosis Rag

(For Rachel, my niece, who taught on Kafka's home turf.)

Manhattan, New York City, April 18, 1924.

As Franz Kafka awoke one morning from uneasy dreams, he found himself transformed in his bed into a writer of musical comedies on Broadway in New York City. As he shook his head, he kept hearing the music coming from the piano, and he wanted to drift off, back to sleep, but duty called once more.

Franz was working with George Gershwin for three months, getting the job as a freak accident after George's brother, Ira, had died, struck by a taxi while stepping out of another taxi. Franz was in the taxi that hit George's brother, and, as one thing led to another, George soon hired the young Franz, new to America, as his new collaborator.

"You write the lyrics, Franz, and I'll write the music," George again told his protégé that morning, just like the other mornings. "What storyline have you dreamed up for me today?"

George was a handsome young man, a genius composer, who could transform any lyrical story into a rollicking sequence of songs that filled an audience with joy and laughter. George Gershwin's Russian Ukrainian Jew hair was black, like Franz's Czech Jew hair, but his body was filled out and robust, while skinny Franz, a vegetarian, looked wan and tired most of the time.

"I have a story in mind about a salesman in New York who wakes up to discover he is transformed into an insect—let's say a beetle. His parents are home, as is his sister, but his great fear arrives when his boss comes over to see why he hasn't reported to work."

"That's hilarious! You have such a vivid imagination, Franz. I can hear the tune now. A jazzy little number, we can call it the *You Bug Me Rag*, you know, a little Scott Joplin, a little Mozart. Something the kids can dance to." George let his hands play over the keys for a few moments, and the notes he struck were indeed a rag-time beat, full of lighthearted and playful riffs. "Now, what does

1

this fellow think, Franz? Let me hear it from his point of view, so I can get an idea of what music to add."

Franz knew whichever words he came up with would be transformed from what he believed to be his dream-like, existential torture into George's romantic comedy energy. They were both very satisfied with their partnership, but Franz's artistic temperament kept him suffering inside.

"All right. Just hold on a moment. These words don't grow on trees—even in Brooklyn." Franz knew his word play would amuse his partner and slow him down. He watched George as he kept up the ragtime beat on the piano, his head bobbing, and his shoulders weaving to the tune. *Oh, God!* Franz thought. *What have I become? First, I have to learn English, the worst language in the world, and now I work for Mister Russian Romance of Brooklyn.*

Finally, after Franz held his tortured head in his hands for fifteen minutes, he began to speak:

I woke up this morning from a lucid dream, but when I moved, I had to scream.

Lying in bed, right on my back. As I inspect, I can see, the eight flailing legs of a giant insect!

George let out a whoop, and his ragtime tune picked up speed. "Amazing, brother! You got it now! Let's hear the chorus."

Daddy won't ever leave me alone, and Mama, when she saw me, spilled coffee on the rug.

If your boss sees you stuck in your room, you better learn to sing, or you'll die, like a bug.

"Yeah, I get the story! This guy, what's his name?"

"Gregor. Gregor Samsa," Kafka reluctantly admitted.

"Poor Gregor. He has to learn to sing in order to become transformed from being just a lonely bug. You know, we all feel like a dumb bug schmuck when we wake up in the big city. Ready to be stepped on the minute we walk outside the door. But what's the female interest, though, Franz? We need some romance." George pleaded; his hands outstretched to his partner like Al Jolson.

"Well, I was thinking that his sister might try to help him. You know, feed him something. And then his father gets angry at Gregor and begins to throw apples at him. One sticks in his back and

2

festers there, and he gradually grows weaker, while everybody in the house, including the lodgers, get tired of him hanging from the ceiling and climbing the walls, but his sister still feeds him, until even she believes he is not her brother. The apple finally infects his back and, well, he dies." Franz saw by the drooping jaw on George's face that he didn't like it. "Or, I could change it. I was thinking about the image of the apple, the Garden of Eden, you know, Genesis? Forbidden fruit?"

"Oh dear, brother! You lost me on that one. We can't have a romance with a sister, now can we? Incest ain't best on Broadway. No, let's say it's the beautiful young maid who works there. She's from a poor family in Brooklyn, but she knows how to dance and sing. She's a flapper in her off hours, you know, the Jazz Age. She can be the one to feed Gregor the Bug Man. At first, she sings a song or two to get him out of the bed, and then they can do a Charleston— yeah that's it! They can cut a rug together—ha, ha—the rug-cutter bug, and then, you know, one thing will lead to another. Love finds a way. Like Beauty and the Beast. The boss can be the villain, and your daddy can also be a louse, okay, but mama and the maid better get together at the end to get old Greg out of his terminal funk and out of his shell, so to speak. It will be a real show-stopper, Franz! You've done it again. I think it'll be better than *The Trial of Joseph K*. People were singing those songs on the subway, I heard them myself. If only Ira were here to see it all." George cried a few tears, but he soon got back to pounding out music on his piano for the new Broadway smash hit.

They called this new musical *The Metamorphosis Rag*. As George predicted, this was also a big hit on Broadway. It would run for two years, and George added it to his list of successes. His first national hit song, "Swanee," was followed by a less successful but superb one-act Jazz Opera, *Blue Monday*. George was a prolific composer, and he enjoyed his partnership with many famous lyricists, including William Daly, Buddy DeSylva, Irving Caesar, Ira Gershwin, and of course, Franz Kafka.

It was in late May of that year of 1924 that Franz came down with a chest cold that was later diagnosed as advanced Tuberculosis, or Consumption, which was the common euphemism. His friend and

3

sometimes collaborator, George, discovered from Franz that he had come to America because of his condition, hoping that American doctors could cure him. Alas, when the young Franz finally had enough money from his songwriting to go to a physician, the doctor informed him that his lungs were so badly infected that Franz would have to be quarantined by law.

Because of his state of contagion, Franz never mingled in public, living in dreaded fear that he would pass along his disease through physical contact. His relatives in Prague were sympathetic, and even his youngest sister, Ottla, offered to come to America to be with him. Franz, who was ever the suffering artist, refused, and instead, he called for his new friend and collaborator, George Gershwin, who was becoming very wealthy from his recent work and long-running musical plays and concerts. Sadly, Franz was not making enough from the small royalties he received from his musical comedies to afford to place himself into a secluded sanitorium for the rich in upstate New York.

"What can I do for you, my friend?" George asked, his dark eyes taking in the fragile body of his one-time collaborator. Kafka was wretchedly thin, his arms like twigs, his legs like a wooden puppet's, and his head displaying the skeletal structure of his forehead, cheek bones, chin, and eye sockets. This framework of bone protruded against his olive complexion like a demon attempting to escape its elastic cage.

"Can you place me in a room … where I can see the people of New York? I came to America … because I had always dreamed of it. This was where anything … was possible … and I wanted to see for myself. Now, at the end of my life, I want to put on … my last show … for these people." Kafka's words came in hesitant gasps, and George had to lean forward in his chair beside the bed to hear him.

George Gershwin at first thought he might place his friend in his high-rise apartment above Manhattan. However, that would only give poor Franz a bird's eye view of the ant-like crowds below. Suddenly, he had a brilliant idea. When George first began in the music business, he had played the piano behind the glass cages of department stores like Macy's and Gimbels. His job was to hawk

4

the sheet music of his publisher in Detroit. The people on the sidewalk out front would tell the runner outside what they wanted to hear played, and he would get it for them and give the sheet music to George, who then would begin playing it inside his display cage. The job was called "song plugger."

"I am going to place you inside a glass viewing room at Macy's Department Store. You will choose the work of writing you most want to represent your life, and I will compose a piece of music, on the spot, which will memorialize you for the ages!" George smiled at Franz, his fellow immigrant, and they were both pleased.

"What about the health inspectors? Will they allow such an insane performance?" Franz asked.

"I'll take care of that. We'll have nurses and doctors on hand, and I'll get a professional reader to present your chosen piece. You will be able to watch the faces of this public you crave, and you can spend your final moments as you wish. I promise I will write a work that will accompany your reading and make you remembered for all time! I know, Franz, that you have not been happy doing musical comedies with me, but they did keep you employed in America. Now you can be known for the secret work I know you've been writing on your own. I know your friend in Czechoslovakia, Max Brod, wants to publish your work, and I'll send it to him after … you know … when you pass." Tears were streaming down George's cheeks as he watched his friend smile in gratitude.

***

Manhattan, Macy's Department Store, New York City, June 3, 1924.

From his vantage point in the bed, Franz could see his friend, George Gershwin, outside, on the sidewalk, his Steinway & Sons grand piano standing regally amongst the crowd of viewers like a wooden soldier. Gershwin began playing his new composition, and the sounds it made captivated the audience, which must have been in the hundreds or perhaps a thousand or more. The spring air was pure and delicate, giving each watcher of the window a breath of freshness that could be held inside the lungs and savored much more because the man in the bed was dying of the disease that made breathing a tortured exercise in futility.

Franz was thinking about the time in 1916 and 1917 when he stayed in a small bungalow on Golden Way near Prague Castle. He began his incomplete novel *The Castle* there, and the memory filled his senses with the bright pastel colors of the buildings, and the odors of flowers and the bakeries in the neighborhood. These buildings used to house the King's alchemists during the Middle Ages. As an artist, Franz was an alchemist of words, forever trying to concoct a mixture that might attract the attention of his Highness in the castle. It was not possible, of course, as he was a lowly Jew, and the king was the king, filled with white goodness and the power of the soldiers and merchants who did his bidding.

But it was springtime, as it was now, and Franz looked from his window at the passing crowds, who knew not what form of creation this imprisoned young man was concocting in his delirium of absurdity. "I must go to America," Franz had whispered in the early morning dawn when the oppressive shadow of that castle filled him with the urge to escape.

Now, as he was dying in his newly discovered paradise, his mind wandered back to that little shelter on Golden Way. He was always similar to what the reader outside the display windows was now reading, "A Hunger Artist," and his friend, George, was also a hunger artist. Franz knew the fantasy could all end at once, a tumor on the brain, a bacillus in the lungs, a war, a fall, a metamorphosis, a microsecond of madness.

This void, Franz understood, was the wellspring of all art, and even the melancholic artists, like George and Franz, knew its silent source of grief for their people, the Jews, the persecuted minorities, the Negroes, the Chinese in California, as each group had its pressures to succeed, to make America greater than she deserved, to cast a shadow of its greatness all over the world. This American shadow, Franz now realized, was possibly more destructive than the Prague Castle back home, and its succession of kings and dictators who would look out its windows down at the people, as Franz was doing now, and attempt to keep them happy for a time with the ephemeral distraction called "art."

Kafka knew, as he took his final, agonizing breaths, and listened to George play his new composition, *Rhapsody in Blue*, as it filtered through the ears of the listening, he was a mere distraction to the citizens of the City of New York. As the final paragraphs of "A Hunger Artist" were read over the loudspeaker to George's brilliant accompaniment, Franz listened carefully to his own words, read by the talented young actor, Orson Welles:

Many more days went by, however, and that too came to an end. An overseer's eye fell on the cage one day and he asked the attendants why this perfectly good cage should be left standing there unused with dirty straw inside it; nobody knew, until one man, helped out by the notice board, remembered about the hunger artist. They poked into the straw with sticks and found him in it. 'Are you still fasting?' asked the overseer, 'when on earth do you mean to stop?'

'Forgive me, everybody,' whispered the hunger artist, only the overseer, who had his ear to the bars, understood him.

'Of course,' said the overseer, and tapped his forehead with a finger to let the attendants know what state the man was in, 'we forgive you.'

'I always wanted you to admire my fasting,' said the hunger artist.

'We do admire it,' said the overseer, affably.

'But you shouldn't admire it,' said the hunger artist.

'Well then we don't admire it,' said the overseer, 'but why shouldn't we admire it?'

'Because I have to fast, I can't help it,' said the hunger artist.

'What a fellow you are,' said the overseer, 'and why can't you help it?'

'Because,' said the hunger artist, lifting his head a little and speaking, with his lips pursed, as if for a kiss, right into the overseer's ear, so that no syllable might be lost, 'because I couldn't find the food I liked. If I had found it, believe me, I should have made no fuss and stuffed myself like you or anyone else.' These were his

7

last words, but in his dimming eyes remained the firm though no longer proud persuasion that he was continuing to fast.

At the moment of his death, Franz Kafka was consoled by the thought that his friends, George Gershwin and Max Brod, would protect his creations and that his final opus, in the window of Macy's Department Store, would not become a musical comedy on Broadway. Or would it?

The Annulment

Blessing of the Night

*I am, beloved, God's narrow mirror, into which he looks, before he
goes to rest.
My heart is the red seal of his ring, which he impresses in the
evening, before he has entirely passed away.*

*I am, beloved, God's silver cup, from which he often drinks the
slumber of red wine,
From whose deep foundation, as from a valley of the pale moon,
the song of melancholy.*

*I was, beloved, God's dumb mirror.
Now, in the distance, I sang songs
To the sound of the stars.*

*My heart was God's seal.
Now he speaks to me from the silence of the stars:*

*A*s Josef, my husband, calls me, I consider who I am.*

"Pepa, I'll be there momentarily. I want to finish writing
this."

*My brother saw me as his comrade and his beloved. One of
his favorite expressions, when he wrote to me, was, 'The first hour
of the first fine day belongs to you.' Indeed, I tried to be his comrade
in most things, such as our shared vegetarian lifestyle, no alcohol,
our stubborn insistence upon helping the outcasts and the poor, and,
most of all, our perpetual war against our father, the first dictator,
Herr Hermann Kafka.*

*My brother always said that my marriage to a Czech
Catholic was worth more than marrying ten Jews. Having a Gentile
husband was like being inoculated against consumption, which*

tragically took the life of my poor Franz in 1924. My brother spent his entire life trying to find a way to become accepted by the outside. His novels, his stories, his aphorisms, and his personal life, were all spent attempting to find a connection to a force that could protect him from 'the process,' as he termed the slow deterioration of self under the weight of modern society.

But now I am forced to make a choice that my brother never had to make. Franz was always too afraid of commitment to anything. Marriage, family, and society were always a burden to him. I tried going to agricultural school in Zürau to become my own woman, but I failed at that. I married Josef because, like Franz, he was an attorney, and like Franz, he wrote poetry. I'm afraid, however, Josef was also like father, a dictator. Franz never saw the similarity Pepa had to father, even though he thought Josef's poems were too patriotic and called them 'nonsensical songs of martial glory.' Franz would always attempt to poke fun at Pepa and his masculine bravado. He once sent him a postcard from Matliary, the tuberculin sanitarium in the Alps where Franz was staying in 1921. It showed a man on skis looking down the gigantic hill covered in snow. Franz told Pepa that he had just competed in the downhill ski competition, and he had a friend take the picture for the cover of the postcard. I never had the courage to tell Franz about how Josef's brand of anti-Semitism made me 'his exceptional Jew,' but all the other Jews, of course, were quite weak, selfish, pacifistic, and lazy.

I have one last chance to redeem myself. Do I stay with my family, at age fifty, and put them in danger of being ostracized from the body politic? Or, do I divorce my Catholic husband, lose my two daughters, and thus save them from punishment by the forces out there that would harm them? In effect, I am writing this down as a journal for any person to read, as my brother wrote his fictions, to provide my readers with a life lesson, even if my life is becoming slowly encapsulated inside a minority which has become a scourge to others: Jew.

"Ottla! Come in here at once. We need to talk."

"Of course. I'm coming now. The girls won't be back until five. We should have more than enough time to discuss our problem."

THE ANNULMENT

***

J Josef "Pepa" David sat in his chair near the table with the radio. With no more soccer games being played because of the war, all he had was his work at the bank and the news on the radio, which was now blasting out, in German, into the living room. Since the occupation began, in 1939, when Hitler spoke from Prague Castle, Josef began his love/hate relationship with the Third Reich. On the one hand, as a former soldier in the First World War, Josef was one of the thousands of Czech troops who defected on the Russian front lines, refusing to fight for Germany and Hungary. They formed what would later become the Czechoslovak Legion, under the leadership of Josef's fellow Catholic, Tomáš Garrigue Masaryk.

When the Germans took over Prague, Josef and his group of Legion vets cursed the radio as Hitler spoke, vowing to resist the occupation. However, when the Deutschmarks began pouring into his bank, and his salary was increased, Josef began having second thoughts about the new Protectorate of Bohemia and Moravia. The only contention left to argue, according to Josef, was Hitler's Nuremberg Laws and how they apply to the Jews and his family.

"Please, turn that off." Ottla walked over to stand beside her husband. She knew enough to try to sit in his presence, as he was like her father had been, the "master of the house." Furnished with plain, wartime furniture, with metal and aluminum confiscated, in addition to the dark window shades in case of air raids, the living room resembled a funeral parlor. Josef turned the knob on the radio with a flick of his wrist and stood up, and his head taller position gave him the authority he commanded. He was thin and virile, and he always wore his dark suits and ties, even when at home, as relaxation in appearance was not a part of his demeanor.

"We've been over this before. Your friends have told you. There is no record of you as a Jew because of our marriage before the war. As long as you stay at home, we can live in peace. I can't take care of Vera and Helene by myself." Josef paced the floor, circling his wife, his hands tightly grasping wrists behind his back.

11

"I refuse to live like a caged animal. When Franz stayed with me in Zürau, he wrote an aphorism. A cage went in search of a bird. The Nazis are that cage, and I am that bird. Don't you see, Pepa? They will eventually capture me, and when they do, I will be judged as a Jew who tried to hide from them. What will happen to you when that occurs? Do you think they would permit you to work in a bank? Would our daughters have any chance to live a normal life?"

"The Legion resists in secret! Why can't you and your Jews resist instead of organizing this pacifist group of cowards under that sniveling Edelstein?"

"Jacob Edelstein is no coward! He could have deserted his people in Prague to live in Palestine. His Zionism is working to free us all so that we may evacuate to the Holy Land. I have spoken to him. He told me that if I divorce you, he will be able to place me on a preferential list. The Protectorate is building a Jewish settlement in Terezin. Jacob says that Jews will be allowed to run everything in this community. First, the elderly will be taken care of, and then we will establish a working social framework in which we can live as peaceful civilians, who can practice our culture and our religion without oppression."

"Why is this happening? The laws of the Third Reich— especially the Nuremberg Laws—say that Jews will never be part of German society. Why should it be any different in the so-called Protectorate in Prague?" Josef rarely allowed any argument to be conducted without his becoming a proper devil's advocate. Although he understood the logic of what his wife was saying, he had seen with his own eyes the beatings of the orthodox Jews in the streets, and the confiscation of the shops and the properties of Jews due to the latest policies coming out of Nazi headquarters.

"That's just it. Jacob says we can serve the Germans as cultural workers. They may not want us to live with them in their communities, but they will certainly want to harness all the genius of my people to improve their status in the world. Theresienstadt is going to serve as the model for future communities whereby Gentiles and Jews can live cooperatively and in the best interests of both. He's also going to keep working to get passports for us to

Palestine. My brother always wanted to go there, but he died. You know he wanted to live there, Pepa."

"Is Edelstein going to provide me with a cook and nanny? I still have to live here, you know, with all these thugs in charge!"

"Don't be absurd. I know you have never understood Zionism or my culture. What I want to offer you will not only protect you and our children, it will also give you the full share of my parents' estate. I will sign it over to you so the Germans can't confiscate it when I turn myself in."

Josef took hold of his wife's shoulders and stared into her brown eyes. She had the same intense gaze that her brother had, but it also held the kindness and sacrifice that Josef David never understood. He did recognize that he was losing a companion and a wife of twenty-two years, but his lawyer mind was working as well. Whereas his brother-in-law, Franz, would always jibe him about his attitude toward the "lazy and poor Jewish refugees," Josef held onto his conservative beliefs, like a dog with his bone.

"Good. I accept your reasoning. How soon will you have to leave us? You can get the divorce tomorrow, as the Protectorate has expedited such things, but then you will become an official Jewess. I cannot protect you after that."

"Jacob told me he can get me on the list for transport to Terezin on Monday, August third. If you don't mind, I would like Vera and Helene to escort me. It will be the last time I will see them until Jacob and the Elders can get us all passports to the Holy Land."

"Of course! But I will not go, Ottla. I don't want to get on any more lists. The resistance will be working to free you all, and it may be us who will rescue you from that Fascist community of yours. I don't have the trusting heart that you have. You keep mentioning your brother, Franz. He may have been a bleeding heart for the poor, but he never had the trust in humanity that you have. According to his philosophy, we all live in a private hell that can never be protected by the Law or by the Castle. You should read his books more carefully."

"My brother was a Zionist when he died. He knew we would need to fight to protect our culture. Will you not move to Palestine if Jacob and the Elders can gain permission?"

13

"I will cross that bridge when we come to it. I agree with your brother in one of his aphorisms. I have it engraved on a plaque and placed upon my desk at the bank. It reads, 'I write differently from what I speak, I speak differently from what I think, I think differently from the way I ought to think, and so it all proceeds into deepest darkness.' My love, I am afraid you are now headed into that darkness."

***

*M*y daughters will not take this well. We have sheltered *them from these kinds of things, and I suppose it's mostly my fault. I have only recently been in contact with the larger Jewish community, so Vera and Helene have been brought up as Catholic all their lives, attending Mass with us to keep the officials from our door. Josef has always kept up with the legal developments in Germany, so he was well aware of the 1935 Nuremberg Laws under Hitler's regime.*

Jacob Edelstein is also aware of the Germans and their laws. Shortly after he was appointed Elder of the Jewish Council in Terezin, he announced his plan to the other elders and the entire community at the Old-New Golem Synagogue. He told us that Hitler and the SS want to use the Jews for cheap labor, and as long as we prove indispensable to their war effort, we will remain valuable. He also said he would be working to get us passports to Palestine, about which he has worked with them before the war. He has the contacts and the methods to do it successfully. I have not told my husband about his secret plan that includes me. Frankly, I don't want him getting drunk and letting it out at the beer hall.

Jacob told me that the Germans always work through hierarchies of power. This includes us, the Jews, who will be their prisoners. The highest in the Jewish prisoner hierarchy are, of course, the thirteen elders who make up the Jewish Council. Among its prisoner population, those Jews who were married to Aryans, such as I, are at the top, along with German military war heroes, and certain important skilled workers.

THE ANNULMENT

Since Jacob has worked most of his life with the Jewish youth, he believes the key to our success is to educate and train all of our young so that they'll be able to work hard for everyone to gain our passports to freedom, which will be our reward. Even if some of the lower-ranking prisoners don't get passports, he will be working hard to negotiate the release of the prisoners who are in the upper echelon of our community.

We'll be training the others to take our jobs, and the Germans will have a constant replenishment of new workers to fill the positions left behind after we've made Aliyah to the Holy Land. The Germans will get the productivity of our hard work, and then they will no longer have us living in Czechoslovakia. The Jews will have a new homeland, and the Germans will have their racial purity. I must admit. There is a certain genius to his plan. Jacob told me I will be working in the main barrack with the girls. Male and female will be separated to ensure productivity, although I understand human nature, and the social reality will be quite different, one would suspect.

I love writing near the window. I have always been like my brother in that we need the vision of Nature to channel our thoughts, no matter how absurd, dark or frivolous. In the end, the frivolity of life wins, although we may not. Just imagine all the infinite reality of existence. Our little planet does not suffice to make us whole. We must always join in the miracle of the never-ending process of God's glory. It is not a moral question.

My poor brother and, to an even greater extent, my husband, both need the finite with which to grapple, and they quickly lose patience with the infinite. I believe most men obsess over the finite all around us. They want to argue it out, provide a conflict, a reason for a fight, or an existentially absurd obstruction. We, women, have always been the peacemakers, attempting to create a path of communications between everything—not just the rich and powerful—and to see the glorious, infinite possibilities in each blade of grass, each child of sentient beings, and the momentary pause that it takes to recognize that one needs a violent act to create evil. We should never kill over land, religion, or culture, but it happens constantly.

15

THE ANNULMENT

It is not the war around me that frightens me most. It is the constant insistence that might makes right and that power is the ultimate answer to differences in opinion. Wars begin from this, and unless we treat the underlying problem, war will remain forever a symptomatic means to an end. The underlying problem is the desire to force others to do our will. Hitler's opus presupposes that it was his will alone that was able to triumph over his adversities. Never does one's lonely will become a victor without the peaceful cooperation and help of others of all differences and all walks of life.

***

The Stromovka Park Trade Fair Grounds is waiting for Ottla and her family to finish their last goodbyes. The Industrial Palace, which was built in 1891 for National Jubilee Exhibition, served as the memorial to Prague's entry into world commerce. Today, in 1942, the flags of the Third Reich and the Protectorate of Bohemia and Moravia, fly on poles on either side of the Palace entrance, with its bombastic Art Nouveau spires and two columns, padded with green rotundas at the top, and the metal grating—like the teeth of an industrial monster--covering the frontage of the clock and the space between the columns. This grand structure all faces forward, at attention, as one comes into the park as if welcoming human progress and the blitzkrieg at the same time.

The place where Ottla David-Kafka will go, along with the other Jews scheduled for transport by train to Bohusovice, is a small lot enclosed with a brick fence topped with barbed wire. It is located some 100 kilometers from the Industrial Palace. This small abyss, in the center of town, informs all visitors with a sign that states, "Attention! All Jews Transported Here! All Others Keep Out!"

***

Vera and Helene were having a tug-of-war with the photo album. Each wanted to choose the pictures their mother would be taking with her to Terezin.

16

Ottla was slowly and methodically placing the vital personal items she was taking with her into a small valise. It had a flowered pattern and opened wide with polished wood clasps in the center. It had been her mother's, who had used it when she took weekend trips with Hermann to visit relatives in Berlin. As her kin behaved nervously, Ottla was calm.

Josef was fiddling with some kind of shoe polish, testing it with his finger, smelling it, and then cursing under his breath. "This won't do, dammit! You'll be slogging through those damned puddles at the Bohusovice train station. Your shoes must be waterproofed!"

Ottla saw the first vision of her brother, Franz Kafka, as she was hugging her husband goodbye. She looked over Pepa's shoulder, and there he was. He appeared as the young man of the days she spent with him in Zürau, where she was living during her attempt to become a farmer. Tuberculosis hadn't taken a firm hold on his body, and he was the same thin, smiling, and relaxed brother who made her heart fill with joy when she was with him. He wore a dark suit, white shirt, and tie.

As a man, Franz had always been the exact opposite of their father. Whereas Hermann was strict with the servants at home and with the employees at their family's store, calling them "lazy louts," and "thieves behind my back," Franz would always smile and ask them how their families were doing and if he could do anything to help them on the job. In a way, Ottla had always believed she let her brother down when she dropped out of agricultural college and married Josef.

"Ottla! What are you staring at? You have to be at the Fairgrounds in an hour, so you had better get going. Girls, take your mother's valise."

The blonde, older girl of 21, Vera, brought the collection of photographs over and stuffed them into the valise. Both she and her sister, Helene, 19, were wearing yellow summer chiffon dresses, with white lace and brown buttons down the front. Helene most resembled her mother, as she was a bit plump with black hair and those penetrating Kafka brown eyes. However, it was Vera, tall, thin and vegetarian like her mother, who most resembled Ottla's personality. She was constantly bringing home stray animals to take care of, and she always had a food hand-out for the beggars she met on her trips to the store for her mother.

"Mama, we chose the best photographs for you to take. Papa doesn't need them. They are wedding photos and the ones taken just after we were born. And the ones taken when Uncle Franz visited— even the one of him holding me when I was two. You said I would rub my palm on the tip of his nose, and he would make a motor boat sound with his lips."

"Enough! Get going now." Josef walked over to the door, opened it, and held it for his girls. His face became very stern; his forehead, cheeks, and neck reddened, and his upper lip began to quiver slightly. After the girls passed him, and Ottla passed over the threshold, he suddenly grabbed his wife by her shoulders and pulled her body against his. "I will get you out of there, Ottla, my love! I promise. We will fight them until they are run out of Czechoslovakia forever! Yes, and I put candle wax on your shoes. They are now weatherproof, by God!"

Ottla pulled back from her husband, but she was looking beyond him, at the vision of her brother standing there in the middle of the living room. "Forever is a long time, Pepa," she said, and she kissed him, tasting the pipe tobacco and remembering the spring day, in 1920, when he had first kissed her after the theater. Franz had fought with her against their father to allow Ottla to marry the Roman Catholic Gentile. "There are now no more Kafkas left in Prague. My sisters have gone, and now I am the last to go. I will write, my love. The girls will watch after you, I promise."

As the two daughters and their mother, Ottla, walked into the Fairgrounds, they began to mingle with about a thousand other Jews, who were queuing up at the table where all the papers were being processed for the trip to Terezin. Ottla could hear the small talk of the crowd as she stood there, and she could also see her brother, Franz, who was now standing in front of the big steam train engine that would take them all to their destination. As she was married to an Aryan, Ottla got preferential treatment. She was even allowed to take 50 crowns with her, although one of the SS guards told her in German that there were plans to have special money printed for life in the "spa" at Terezin, as he called it. The little Jewish town was to have its bank, its Jewish government, and would represent all that was best, as a gift from *"der Fuhrer*, Herr Adolph Hitler."

"Mama, we want to go with you!" Vera was clutching at Ottla's sleeves. "Papa will just make us work all the time. We'll never get a chance to see anybody. You'll be in your town created just for you!"

The supervisor of the processing center overheard the girls as he was going through Ottla's papers. He had the Hitler mustache, and the two lightning bolts on the collar of his grey uniform, representing an official of the SS, or Schutzstaffel. He smiled at Vera, "Miss, you and your sister are only half Jewesses. One must be one hundred percent, Jew, to live in Theresienstadt spa."

Ottla held both of her daughters in her arms as she bade them farewell. "Vera, you must watch over Helene. You know how she likes to fight and get into trouble, just like her father. One in the family who goes to prison is quite enough for now. I love you both so very much! Make me proud of you. I will write soon, and you must reply immediately to tell me how you are doing in school."

The supervisor stood with Ottla's daughters, as they were now crying, as the fifty-year-old mother climbed aboard the train into the first car. There was room enough for all, and it was quite hot, being August, but everybody on board was polite and optimistic, as they were the preferred group of Class A prisoners. As she settled into her seat next to the window, however, Ottla again saw the image of her brother, who was now looking up at her, standing directly beneath the car she was now in. He was not smiling. His stare was the way he always looked at her whenever she had to get up at seven in the morning to be the first to open the family's haberdashery. Franz knew his ten-year-old sister would be spending eight to twelve hours each day slaving for their father in that store, and he pitied her.

***

*F*rom the first day of my life here in this converted fortress, I have lived in the Magdeburg Barracks where the Jewish Council of Elders resides. I see one or more of the elders

19

every day, on my way from my new home or upon returning from my job in the Girls' School in Building L-410 located next to the Catholic Church on Hauptstrasse, the main street of the ghetto. This was the home for Jewish girls from 8 to 16 years of age. The older girls, aged 14 to 16, had to work during the day, but still took classes at night. When I pass an elder, he will always address me by name, in German, as this is the language of the upper classes here.

Yes, and Franz's ghost (I no longer believe he is simply a hallucination) is here with me, and we are on speaking terms since the first day my class of girls was deported on a train headed east. The official word from the Council of Elders, who were responsible for making the lists for the Germans and the SS, was that the children were going to the new 'Family Camp' that had been constructed in Auschwitz-Birkenau Camp in Poland, where they would continue their education while their parents worked. When Paul Eppstein told me this, I heard laughter behind him. Standing in the corner was my brother, Franz, and he was laughing uproariously at what Eppstein was telling me. I waited until Eppstein left my bedroom cell in Magdeburg Barracks before I spoke to Franz, who was still standing there, perhaps a bit evanescent, yet still real.

'Why do you laugh? Indeed. Why are you here? Are you going to torment me until I die? Isn't it bad enough I can only write 30 words on a postcard to Josef, Vera, and Helene? Now I have to live each day with the ghost of my pessimistic brother?'

Franz smiled his usual condescending grin reserved for me. 'Ottillie. Did you read the Parable of the Law in my novel? The Law that is meant for you is the same law that condemns you to death. The State has the supreme power over its citizens, and we merely attempt to unravel the complex web of lies to find the Truth for our individual life. Can't you see it all for what it is? The Jewish Elders are the puppets of the Nazi puppet master, Herr Hitler. You are existing in his little charade of a ghetto until the call comes down to send Jews to the east. Work will make you free? Work will also kill you! Do you know how many workers died before I invented my hat made of steel for the foundries in Prague? Thousands each year! I was given a bonus of 100 Crowns from my employer, the Workmen's

Accident Insurance Institute, for my invention. Did my invention save me from being cut down in my early youth by disease? No! But it did allow more steel to be forged to build the monstrous machines of war and the buildings of capitalistic gamblers who keep the profits away from those hard-hatted puppets inside those stifling foundries of Hell. Many millions more could die on the battlefields and from the work, so my contribution meant little in the end. The clock ticks for you, alone, my love. Don't let these puppet Jews make you believe in their charade. It will, alas, eventually mean the death of you!'

Franz disappeared, but his words stayed with me all that week until I was told a story by a woman who played the piano for all the concerts held in the Culture House on Langestrasse. Her name was Alice Sommer, and she was the most beautiful person I have ever met. Not just her physical beauty, mind you, as she was not a film star beauty; it was her person, her spirit, and the way she looked at life that made me love her almost instantly. She wore a long blue dress and pearls around her neck. Her dark hair and eyes penetrated mine the way Franz's always did, but in a different way. My brother always made me feel as if he were ripping the flesh off my bones to leave my white skeleton. Alice's gaze felt like a penetration into my very soul.

She had lived in Prague but spoke German, mostly, and her mother was very intellectual, so she was able to meet many famous people, including Sigmund Freud, Gustav Mahler, Franz Werfel, and, as she informed me that day, my older brother.

'Kafka was a slightly strange man. He used to come to our house, sit and talk with my mother, mainly about his writing. He did not talk a lot but rather loved quiet and nature. We frequently went on trips together. I remember that Kafka took us to a very nice place outside Prague. We sat on a bench and he told us stories'

I asked her how she was getting on in the ghetto, and she smiled. She was able to live with her son, Raphael, in a private cell, and most of her relatives were able to escape to Palestine before the war. Her husband, Leo, was sent to Dachau. When I asked her about how she liked giving concerts in the hall, she lit up like an air-raid searchlight and said, 'We have to play because the Red Cross will come three times a year. The Germans want to show their representatives that the situation of the Jews in Theresienstadt is good. Whenever I know that I have a concert, I am happy. Music is magic. We perform in the council hall before an audience of 150 old, hopeless, sick, and hungry people. They live for the music. It is like food to them. If they weren't able to come to hear us, they would have died long before.'

When I told her about my class of girls being deported to the east, she just nodded her head slowly, and said, 'What did you do with them, Ottla?'

'I just taught them the basics. You know, how to add and subtract. How to read with emotion.'

'Knowledge is also sweet, like candies. The appreciation of what you did for them will be seen in their daily lives as they find the skills useful. Whether they think about you, or not, what you gave them will be with them forever.'

'But, forever is the problem, Frau Sommer. What if the rumors are true? What if the Nazis are sending our children to their deaths?'

Alice Sommer stopped smiling, and yet there was that magic glittering in her blue eyes. 'In God's mind, there is no time. Herr Einstein says it's true, no? We impose limits on the time that doesn't exist. Therefore, the quality of time spent becomes more important than how long it lasts, does it not? The highest mitzvah is the good deed we do that is completely anonymous. The only credit we receive is in the act of making magical music or teaching the magical knowledge to the young ones. If our audiences appreciate us for that time, then it is rewarding enough. If they do not, then they must have a personal reason for doing so, and it is in God's hands, nevertheless. Yahushua oversees eternity. Never forget that, young lady!'

Alice Sommer invited me to come to the theater that night to watch a play written by another Kafka, whose name was Georg. As it turned out, he was a distant cousin of ours. The play being presented was a one-act feature called 'The Death of Orpheus.' I told her I would be very happy to attend, even if it was just to be able to see her once again. We kissed, and I was balanced once *more, tilting away from my brother's pessimism, like a sunflower that moves with the sun.*

***

At the presentation of *The Death of Orpheus*, Ottla sat next to her new friend and spiritual mentor, Alice Herz-Sommer. Most prisoners were never able to get a ticket to the Cultural Theater. However, the songs, the plays, and the concerts were memorized and repeated by the fortunate Jews who were able to attend, so that there was a constant recreation of what had transpired, giving those outside the preferred minority a brief taste of joy. Most of the plays were comedies and musicals, and there was even a jazz band. That evening, when a fifty-one-year-old divorcee and mother, Ottla David-Kafka, became mesmerized by the twenty-one-year-old playwright and actor, Georg Kafka, the play was a tragedy.

Ottla could not take her eyes off the young man playing Orpheus on the stage. Except for his curly black hair, he could have been the twin of her Franz. As her eyes moved from the stage to the corner where the musicians were accompanying the presentation, she saw her brother's ghost once more. He was standing directly behind the cellist, a famous musician who used to play for the Prague Philharmonic. The cello was always Franz's favorite instrument, as he said it produced the "chords of sadness" that his heart contained. It was the final scene, and Georg was seated on the floor of the stage, his head down, his arms enveloping his head as if he were ensnared in some kind of trap. As the cello played, a gift of a golden lyre is handed to our hero on stage by a servant. It is from his lost love, Eurydice, who was banished to the Underworld when she made the mistake of looking back as he was attempting to rescue her. In the Bible, Lot's wife looks back at Sodom and Gomorrah and is changed into a pillar of salt.

Ottla believed those women in Terezin, who looked back to Prague or their former lives, were also cursed in some cruel way. Her daily postcards to her daughters were tiny daggers that tore into her heart, as she knew she could not see them, touch them, or hear their voices. There was nothing—even art—that could replace the joy of being in person with the ones you love.

This was what the young man's one-act play was all about. Earlier in the play, Orpheus' mother tries to talk him back to life, but it does not work, but the gift of the lyre tears into Orpheus's melancholy state of mind, and he immediately jumps up and begins to play. A frenzy of music and dancing ensues, until from the wings of the stage, come the wild women, the Maenads, the followers of Dionysus, the Greek god of fertility, wine, and art. They cavort in turmoil around Orpheus, tearing at his toga with their hands, screaming in ecstatic passion, until the lights die down, leaving Orpheus dying and alone. However, the light shines upon the golden lyre, leaving Orpheus alone in his agony, and providing the audience with the final image of hope.

When Alice introduced Ottla to the young actor and playwright following his production, it was he who became entranced. "You are Ottla Kafka? Was your brother Franz?" When she nodded, he became immediately animated. "He is the greatest artist of the century! He predicted the rise of the totalitarians, and his novel, *The Trial*, shows how one person can be judged guilty just for being born, just as Jews are being judged today. What a prophet he was!"

"Yes, but you didn't have to live with him," Ottla smiled. "I'm afraid much of what my brother wrote was probably because of his insecurities and fears. True. I supported his art, and I saw in it a value that went beyond time, but he may have been haunted more by the goals he could not accomplish while he was alive. Speaking of being alive, what do you do when you're not on stage dying the agonizing torture of the lovelorn?"

"I teach the boys. I was a teacher before I was arrested, so they gave me this job to do. My mother, Sarah, is with me as is my father."

"Do you believe the rumors concerning the eastern camps? That they are nothing more than death camps and that the Nazis are killing Jews by the thousands every day?"

"I believe in the wisdom of your brother's story, 'In the Penal Colony.' Did you read it?"

Ottla nodded in the affirmative.

"When the State gives its bureaucratic members the power over life and death, as the head of the penal colony has in the story, the act of killing with precision and skill becomes more important than the person being killed. Therefore, your brother, in all his genius, spends much more time and attention describing how the death machine works than he does describing the victim and whether his criminal act was worthy of the death penalty. In other words, once the order has been given to kill, some will follow orders no matter what."

"Yes, Franz worked at an accident insurance company. He was forever going over the blueprints of machines that ran in the factories all over Prague. In his business, it was not so important to protect the worker from accidents as it was to reduce the cost of injuries that the company had to pay. The machine of Capitalism always trumped the machine of the human being."

"That's why we are so fortunate to be in Terezin. The Germans need us to show a good face to the world. The International Red Cross visits, and we are told to act as if we are always well fed and are living the life of luxury. It is all a drama, and I should know what drama is! But is not all of life a stage, as Shakespeare called it? Frau Sommer said you were teaching in the camp. My children have also been sent on trains to the east. Would you like to assist me in my attempt to determine what is happening to our children?"

"You mean, you want to spy on the Council of Elders?" Ottla's voice was a whisper.

"I am also a courier for the Council and that gives me access to their offices and other places around the two fortresses. I have uncovered some information that casts light upon the way lists are created for the deportations. But now I want to see if another fact I have uncovered is true."

"What fact?"

"Meet me tomorrow with your dinner ration coupon at the dining hall. I'll be standing at the first pillar as you go in. I shall tell you then. There are too many Nazis around here tonight." Georg turned his head toward the side of the Culture Theater where four

25

uniformed SS Guards stood smoking. No prisoners could smoke, so these men looked like a collection of chimneys in a circle.

"All right. I will be there. This adds some excitement to our lives, as did your play. I thank you, Cousin Georg, for both."

Georg took Ottla's right hand and brought it to his lips. "My heart is God's seal," he told her.

"How so?" she asked.

"It's from a poem I am writing. I tell my students that God places His seal upon our hearts so that we can know we are His children forever."

"That's beautiful! You do have the soul of the poet. My brother would have enjoyed meeting you. However, the seal he would point out is the star we have to wear."

***

*A*s *Ottla David-Kafka awoke one morning from uneasy dreams, she found herself transformed in her bed into a gigantic butterfly. This is how I want to describe my life after meeting Georg and Alice. As you can see, I have taken my brother's famous opening line from his novella 'The Metamorphosis,' and transformed it to suit my authorial purposes in this journal. Herr Goebbels, the Nazi Minister of Propaganda, has called Jews 'vermin' to be eradicated, so my brother was prophetic when he used this word in his story. However, because I am living my days in Theresienstadt, 'Hitler's Gift to the Jews,' the insect I have metamorphosed into is much more appropriate to the process my brother was supposedly describing. In the actual act of metamorphosis, the caterpillar must first become the pupa encased in his shell. Then, during the miraculous incubation, the insect changes into the beautiful winged Monarch, Painted Lady, Goliath Birdwing or Blue Morpho. My brother's metamorphosis never takes place! Thanks to God, mine did.*

My life as a butterfly began on the day following. I met Georg at the dining hall, under the first pillar. He did not remark upon my wings, and I did not choose to use them, as yet, but I do believe some of my powdery residues got on his lapels because he brushed them off with his hand. He told me he had reason to believe that the leader of the Jewish Council of Elders, Jacob Edelstein, was behind the transports of both the elderly and the children to the east.

After eating, I journeyed with him to the office of Edelstein. I believed my heart's joy was going to be brief, as is the time on this Earth of the butterfly, and I wanted to enjoy every second I could of this new life. Even when he handed me the written proof that our elder leader had planned out the dietary rules of the ghetto, and he had also signed off on the transports of the elderly and children to the east, I still didn't believe these were evil acts. Georg said, 'Come with me,' and that's when I was taken to the large fortress, where I saw how the elderly were living.

We knew our little paradise for the Jews was a charade. We worked in civilian clothes, yet the Jewish star was on the pockets of our coats. We believed our Czech leader, Edelstein, was in charge, but the fact was that Herr Eichmann had given two other Jews, Paul Eppstein of Berlin, and Benjamin Murmelstein of Vienna, more power over the choice of who was deported. Therefore, more Czech Jews were being deported by the Council, and as I saw, our grandmothers and grandfathers were being slowly starved to death, and they lived in damp, disease-ridden squalor inside the basement of that fort. I saw it with my own eyes. Distinguished Czech war heroes, professors emeritus from universities, doctors, and attorneys, who were now groveling on the ground in the sawdust of the military encampment. Packed into the casements meant for cannons were the bodies of the best Judaism had to offer.

Georg told me that he had seen the orders to the Council that explained how the elderly were being tricked to turn over their fortunes to the Nazi regime before their transport to our ghetto in Terezin. To maintain the illusion for domestic consumption, regional German authorities lulled the elderly, war veterans, and prominent personages with ruses such as home purchase contracts, 'deposits' for rent and board, inducements for future 'residents' to sign life insurance policies over to the German state. All of this money, as the Council knew, would be funneled back into the government of the Jewish Council to improve the living conditions of the young workers. So, this was the humanitarian plan that the great Czech Jew, Jacob Edelstein, had negotiated! Seeing these elders, and how they had to exist, made me sick to my stomach.

My wings, thank God, took me out of there. I flew up into the rafters of the fortress basement, toward the light coming from the transoms, but I could not escape the stench of the dying bodies, their excrement, and I could not stop hearing their cries of tortured agony as they squirmed like disease-infested vermin on the floors of that dark cavern of infamy.

Finally, I found a way to fly out of that room, and I soared, up the stairs, passing other elderly, probably demented, as they wandered about, talking to themselves, to lost relatives, to an angry God who would do this to them.

When I landed, I was in the office of Jacob Edelstein once more. George was opening the locked drawer of his boss's desk from a key he obtained that was hanging on the bedpost inside Edelstein's bedroom in the Magdeburg Barracks. Inside that drawer, Georg extracted three magazines that depicted men having sexual relations with young boys.

When the young teacher turned toward me, my gaze was frozen on those images as if I were being tortured. 'I can see why he might prefer the young over the old,' was what Georg said. This young artist with a pure heart had transformed into the ghost of my Franz! He had that same mocking grin and desperate, penetrating gaze.

I screamed, and I flew out of that room. I began to fly toward the only place where I could keep my sanity. I fluttered down and through the doors of the Cultural Theater. There she was! Alice Sommer was playing the piano, alone, practicing for her next concert. As I flew above her, I watched her hands as they glided over the keys, knowing precisely how to touch them, how to bring the right notes from the piano that would depict the angelic music of Beethoven's Symphony Number Nine, in B minor, Opus 25. The 'Ode to Joy.'

Was this the only place in the world where freedom could exist? Was she the summer of hope inside our insane asylum? I did not know the answer, but I still knew how to fly away to escape the madness of reality. The Embellishment was coming, and the ones who tried to stop it would be sent to the east. The three wise men came from the east to bring gifts for the baby Jesus, the Jew who was to redeem us all. But we, who are still waiting for personal redemption, will have to be satisfied with a seal from God, which marks us as chosen, which marks us to live in a covenant for eternity.

* * *

On All Souls' night inside the city of Prague, two young women are standing by the fire with their father, a law-abiding Catholic gentleman, who watches over his daughters like they are precious jewels. The older daughter, Vera, skips into the center of the living room and fastens her hands on one of the four wooden chairs that have been hauled in from the kitchen earlier by their father.

"This is Mama. See how the cushion glows? I sewed it myself!"

The younger girl, Helena, runs over to another chair and plops her behind on its cushion. "Papa! I am sitting on your spirit!"

The father, Josef, tears in his eyes, wonders what his wife is doing now. He knows she is in the best camp, and he also knows his wife has divorced him. Why does he still miss her? The touch of her tender hand, the warm glow of her dark face as she works in the garden, sews at her machine; all of these memories flood his mind at once.

Divorce you, my Ottla? Never in a million lifetimes!

On All Souls' Day, the living souls are supposed to pray for the spirits of the dead, who have yet to see God, but the spirit of one Ottla David permeates this little home with loneliness and fear. All three of these praying family members take turns sitting in the chair of their missing loved one, and they cry out in agony, and beseech God, as the winds blow snow into drifts on the streets outside, creating barricades of white.

***

Moshe, a blond and blue-eyed little boy, tries to sit up straight the way the driver of the bus sits. He pretends to turn the wheel as the bus rolls down the road. He sees the man turn toward him, and he smiles and holds up his fingers—all of the ones on his right hand and the thumb on his left hand. "I'm six!" Moshe tells the driver.

"That's good! Are you the driver now?" the bus driver asks.

Moshe says nothing, but he stares out through the driver's window at the road and concentrates on his imaginary wheel with all his might. When Moshe sees his parents in the road about to be hit, he screams, "Watch out! Don't hit them!"

The driver again turns toward him and frowns. "What's the matter, little fellow? Are you seeing things that aren't there? It will soon be All Souls' Day, and I guess you're seeing some spirits. Is that it? Do you see ghosts, my little man?"

Moshe nods his head vigorously up and down.

The black bus drives into the camp with the fifty orphaned children of the wealthy. Ottla watches the children as they exit. She smiles. More students. They are soon followed by the trainload of 1,210 other children from poor parents, but they are still orphans, and that is why they are at the best camp of them all in Prague. Only the exclusive citizens are allowed into this camp, and the new Elder Leader, Paul Eppstein, is there with his team of doctors to greet them.

Moshe watches the other children file out of the bus. He doesn't want to leave. He wants to stay with the driver and learn to drive.

When he hears the commotion outside, however, Moshe decides to leave his seat and look at what is happening.

The other children, who are all strangers to Moshe, are stomping their feet, weeping, and trying to run away. The uniformed men are the same ones who were at his parents' house, and Moshe's heart begins to quicken its beats in his narrow chest, as he watches them herd the children.

From the back rows of camp citizens, comes a dark woman with piercing brown eyes and raven hair. She also has a streak of white that runs through it, from the top of her forehead to the end of the long tresses that hang down her back. These people wear fashionable clothing, and Moshe thinks they might be rich like his parents.

The woman speaks to the camp Elder, and he, in turn, speaks to the officers in charge. They all circle away from the hundreds of children, and Moshe can hear them arguing. The Camp Elder tells the dark woman, "Go ahead, Ottla. You tell them.".

The woman speaks to them, and her voice is calm and reassuring. Moshe instantly remembers his own mother's voice, and his heart lessens its frantic pace.

"Children. Because it is All Souls' Day tomorrow, we shall be going on an adventure! Fifty-three of us will accompany you to your new homes in Sweden and Denmark. We shall load you all now, and we will be leaving in two hours. I will meet you inside the train, and we will be on our way." The woman turns to go, and the children all cry out in joy.

Moshe, too, believes this woman, and he promptly gets into the queue that is forming nearest him. His long pants, boots, wool coat, and little grey cap are all he needs.

Ottla quickly writes a postcard to her husband and two daughters: *Es geht mir gut* ("I am fine") it says.

Inside the boxcar, the woman who spoke to the other adults smiles down at Moshe. He sees the silver light from the racing moon shine upon her face through the boxcar's slits. She is a living spirit, and he asks, "Can I drive a bus when we get to Sweden?"

"Yes, you certainly can. What's your name?" she asks him.

"Moshe. Moshe Benjamin Abramowitz," he says. "I'm six."

"Nice to meet you, Moshe. My name is Ottla Kafka David."

***

After many hours, Moshe's eyes slowly open. He stares up at the woman, who is now crying, standing between the open doors of the boxcar. She is facing him, so he can barely make out her features.

Behind her, the moon is full, and below the moon are soldiers standing in the snow. With each soldier is a dog. Each dog is barking loudly, and Moshe puts his hands over his ears to stop the noise. These are the same kinds of dogs that were there on the night they took his parents. Behind it, is a smokestack gushing smoke.

"Lies!" The dark woman screams, and she covers her mouth with both hands, and she sobs into them.

In the corner of the boxcar, as they are all stumbling down the improvised wood ramp, to the snow, Moshe sees a strange man, a very thin man, with dark hair, standing in the cold shadows. The light of the full moon radiates his face. Is he a ghost? He smiles at Moshe, and there is something in that smile that makes the boy feel warm. The boy wonders why this man stays inside the boxcar.

Moshe feels a hand take his. It is once again the dark woman who screamed, and the boy's fear gradually subsides, until they are both standing in a queue leading into the camp beyond. Moshe's eyes are fixed on the snarling dog alongside the queue.

A soldier takes their two hands—the boy's small hand and the dark woman's larger one—and he yanks them apart. Moshe is ordered to go his way, with the other children, to the Children's Camp, "*das kinderlager*," the soldier tells him, and the dark woman goes her way, with the other adults. Moshe supposes his bus driving will have to wait until morning.

Moshe looks up at the full moon, bulging in the sky above everything, and the face he sees on the surface of the yellow moon looks exactly like the man's face he saw inside the boxcar. Again, the boy feels warmth, and so he bravely walks on through the snow and slush.

When he turns around to see where the dark woman who cried was, in the adult queue, Moshe suddenly remembers her name. Ottla. "Ottla!" Moshe shouts into the freezing air. There is no answer, so he turns back around.

Moshe looks up into the night sky once more. The smiling face of the moon man from the boxcar grins down at him, so he does what children and most humans do, he smiles back. "Nice to meet you, sir," says Moshe, and he tips his little cap toward his new friend, and he continues to walk, waiting patiently for the moon man's response. The voice whispers to the boy, from the silence of the stars, "My seal is on your heart, and you are mine … forever."

32

THE ANNULMENT

With this new information, Moshe gains strength, and his steps are made the way he used to see his father make them as he led the family to shul. The boy lifts his feet high, and he takes bold strides, leading these children, who all have seals on their hearts, and who are now his new family, into their *kinderlager*, their new *shul*.

Communion

"To St. Anne, God has given the power to aid in every necessity, because Jesus, her Divine Grandchild according to the flesh, will refuse her no petition, and Mary, her glorious daughter, supports her every request. Those who venerate good St. Anne shall want for nothing, either in this life or the next." —Abbot Trithemius

St. Anne's Hospital, Psychiatric Ward, Fall River, Massachusetts, October 22, 1972.

I can hear Aaron Copeland's *Fanfare for the Common Man* playing a robust accompaniment to my walk across the first floor of the hospital. My chest swells with pride, as the cymbals and kettle drums begin. I know the trumpets will be next, giving me courage, in tandem with the music, to resolutely climb up those sixty-eight creaking stairs to the violent ward and my twin sister, Rose. This is a frequent ritual I have, whenever I'm doing, or am about to do, something that makes me extremely uncomfortable.

God has given me the gift of mentally transporting myself to a previous experience for comfort or escape. In this instance, I am attending a performance of the Fall River Orchestra, who are playing a special summer concert in the city's park. Sitting on the hill's slope of grass, in front of the bandstand, I can feel the energy from the music entering my body. The odor of cotton candy and hot dogs makes my stomach gurgle, and I can see several members of my parish seated on the chairs set up for the special occasion. They are disabled, and two are from St. Anne's. We are all inside my protective memory, enjoying the experience, far from the war raging in Vietnam. Far from my walk up the stairs to the violent ward.

I did this same kind of mental gymnastics the night our mother, Maureen, confronted us. It was just a week after two Army officers came to the door of our house on Spring Street, in June 1944, to tell mother that her husband, and our father, Sergeant Grady O'Bannon, had perished on the beaches of Normandy, during the Allied invasion of France and Italy. She came into the living room from the kitchen. Rose had just kicked all of my little army men into oblivion, and I was shouting at her. Our mother, I realized, was holding something behind her back, and I watched, as she brought her right index finger up to her red lips. "Shhh!" To my child's imagination, what she brought from behind her back looked like the tray the altar boy holds for parishioners during Communion. I knew we were only in kindergarten, and First Holy Communion wouldn't be until Second Grade. Mother brought the tray up to the level of her protruding collar bones. She had not eaten in many days. That's when I saw the black handle on the end of the tray, and I saw her fingers wrapped around it. Her right hand was bone-white from gripping the handle so hard. I then noticed that her other hand was holding the front part of the tray, but, as she pulled the shiny metal toward her, her white neck stretched, like a swan's, as she looked up toward Heaven. My mind transported me, and Bishop Monahan whispered to us, bent over, during our father's Requiem Mass service, and his breath smelled like wine, "The Church will always be here to protect you." The priest walked down the middle of the aisle, toward my father's coffin, as the organist played and the choir sang, *Dies Irae*, and I pulled the incense smoke into my face, as he passed by me, magically thinking it would dry my tears. Our mother shed no tears at our father's funeral nor for that entire week afterward. We finally saw them, glistening on her cheeks, as she pulled the butcher knife into her soul, to stop the lurching sobs erupting from her heaving breast.

Visiting my sister Rose every day is a penance I have to pay. The archdiocese raised us in their orphanage for ten years, after our mother committed suicide, so I felt obligated to continue working for them. They held no Funeral Mass for mother, as they had done for my hero father. She was buried away from the Catholics in the Oak Grove cemetery rather than in St. Patrick's. I have always believed that my becoming a priest gave her death the dignity it deserved. Today, I am a teacher, a Jesuit priest, with a Master's Degree from nearby Stonehill College. My Bishop Connolly High School biology students are some of the brightest in the state, but my inability to communicate with my sister has become my cross to bear. Rose went mad, ten years ago, in 1962, on the October 22nd anniversary of when our mother died, and I felt responsible for my sister's insanity. No physical or metaphysical distraction can protect me from this terror, hiding in my mind's shadows, just out of reach. My relationship with my sister has been severed, I believe, to protect my sanity. I visit Rose to prevent her from going where our mother, so sinfully and selfishly, disappeared. The dates are clear. Ten years. A decade. First, our mother, and, ten years later, my sister went insane. And now, ten years after madness took her, I know Rose is waiting up there, in the violent ward, and I must stop her.

As I touched step number sixty-three, my mind wandered back to that day I confronted Rose, just as mother had confronted us, but my blade was the blade of Truth. In 1962, just before Rose had her nervous breakdown, her new husband, Anthony Nicolosi, the postman, was being unfaithful to her. I tried to tell her about him, but she would never listen.

I could hear that same crow-sized, Pileated woodpecker, as he probed the tall oak like a red-headed surgeon. His communion with the tree began slowly, like the migraines I've been getting lately, and then the explosive "rat-tat-tat-tats" overwhelmed my speech, and I had to speak over the noise. "Three women in the church have confessed to me about affairs they've had with a mailman," I told Rose, seated in our morning breakfast nook, in front of the kitchen window, opening out to the back yard. The archdiocese had given me special permission to temporarily house her in the Jesuit rectory, near the high school, along with her new husband, the mail carrier, Tony. Her passionate green eyes were sparkling, as usual, and I was smoking another one of my nervous, seemingly endless, Benson & Hedges cigarettes. I was wondering if she was stoned on one of her marijuana cigarettes, or "joints," as she called them. I knew I was breaking church doctrine by telling her about what I'd heard inside the confessional, but her use of drugs was just as sinful.

Facing me, she stared ahead, at nothing, and her tanned arms wrapped around the chair back, as if she were welded to it, the way the woodpecker outside was strapped to his tree. Her Gypsy scarf was tied around her forehead, and I could see the outline of her nipples beneath her peasant blouse. I continued, "They told me they were overcome by his handsomeness, so I asked them to describe him." Rose blinked, and those green eyes swiveled toward mine, her head not moving, so I explained to her that this Lothario postman must be Anthony because these women said he had what Rose called "those devil-black eyes" and "those shady palm fronds," or long, Italian eyelashes.

Rose was getting stoned nearly every day back then, in 1962. She began the habit after I graduated from college, in 1960. She told me that a joint made her daily chores much easier to handle, and, at first, I believed her. She bopped to her Elvis, and twisted with Chubby Checker, shaking her long black hair from side-to-side, and wiggling her shapely fanny inside a tropical muumuu. She laughed uproariously at the antics of our cat, a black feline named JFK (after our first Catholic President). JFK hissed, with an arched back, and darted from one hiding place to another, while Rose pushed the "holy terror," the vacuum cleaner, across the rectory floors.

"Those women read too many dime-store Romances. They might dream they're fucking my Tony, but they're just trying to get *you* hard, Father O'Bannon." Rose tossed her head back and howled with laughter until the cat stopped and stared at her. My twin sister knew what to say to get me unnerved. I wish I had been wrong, but when Rose and Tony began to scream and yell, I knew I had been correct, and I prayed I could convince them to go to couples' counseling.

Before I began my first visit to the violent ward, I spoke with the supervisor of the hospital, over the public telephone, on the wall near the stairs. The powerful cymbals and kettle drums of *Common Man* were playing in the background of my thoughts as I listened to her patronizing voice. According to Sister Patriarcha, Mother Superior of St. Anne's Dominican Sisters of the Presentation, "Rose cannot connect any internal hallucination, about which she constantly fantasizes, with the intruding hands that she believes come out of nowhere to prod her, to bathe her, and to feed and dress her. These hands are not people to Rose. These are severed limbs that puncture her, just as violently as the needles she feels in her arm or the electric jolts that tear into her brain during the electroshock treatments. She needs our gentleness and our prayers at this point, Father." I thanked her, but I knew her version of the candid truth was far from the reality. From my years of experience as a pastor, roaming these same lunatic halls, I was well aware of the tricks the mind can play. I was also aware of how long the memory of the Church could last if you didn't measure up to their standards. The image of our Pileated woodpecker came back to my mind's eye, and this time my sister was the tree, and each French-Canadian nun was flying around her, dive-bombing against her paralyzed young body, leaving deep holes and puncture wounds that would never heal. "Take that, you whore of Babylon," one spat in her face and injected her with a sedative. "You're just like your mother, you slut!" another shouted, pressing copper pads against Rose's temples, and then turning up the juice from the electroshock generator. My fantasies were becoming dourer, the closer I came to her tomb within the violent ward.

I knew Rose's schizophrenia precluded her memory of past events, and only the Catholicism around her could recall her sinful ways. My status as a Jesuit priest was the only buffer between Rose's lunacy and their possible cruelty. The reality Rose lived inside today had no referential connection with the Catholic Church's list of rules. I understood that her existential reality was now split-off from what was happening in this sinful world. I knew I must bring her back from the abyss before it was too late. As I placed my size 10 ½ black shoe upon the sixty-eighth step, my mind again transported me back in time.

I was remembering all the other times I had been at St. Anne's, before Rose went insane, to visit some of my parishioners and former students. These people were housed on the first floor, the non-violent floor. As I made my rounds, listening to their tales of bad acid trips, their perverted, homosexual desires, and their seemingly endless list of phobias, I was silently praying to Him for my needed forgiveness. I realized I was ignoring my sister, who was down the street, at Dollie's Pub, working as a Go-Go Dancer. I also realized both she and I were having a personal confrontation with God. Hers ended when she met Anthony, who had enjoyed watching her twist her shimmering hips and stroke her swimming arms within the invisible sea cage surrounding her. When she finally looked down at him, with our green eyes, he began his ritual communion, understanding, with his brute intelligence, her need for sexual intimacy. Rose was my twin, and, in many ways, I share her appetite for madness. I dread this approaching moment with her because, even though my inner yearning is pure, I also realize that I may finally join her in a mad dash toward final escape.

My heart was pounding, so I stopped to genuflect on the padded kneeler near the only wide window on the violent floor, in front of the holy shrine near the reception desk. Enclosed within this enclave, like a womb of serenity, was a tall white statue of St. Anne, holding onto the shoulders of her sacred daughter, Mary, the Mother of Jesus. I prayed that I could rise to this occasion and be forgiven. When I finished my prayer, I rose, and I walked over to the reception desk. The smiling young nun behind it turned toward me and politely nodded.

"Good morning, Father O'Bannon," the nun said as if she knew me personally. I noticed that the white of her teeth matched the snowy color of the Bandeau, which encircled her face, as if a giant Communion wafer had been cut, like a paper doll, to reveal her tempting beauty. I didn't remember her name, as my recent inability to remember any person's name was one of the signals that my brain was sending me, late at night. I decided to strike back at this innocent nun to assuage my fear.

"Did you know, my young sister, that I am reincarnated?

"Reincarnated?" The nun's eyebrows rose along with her voice's tone of incredulity.

"Yes. My brother, in 1532, was murdered while performing his priestly duties. An O'Carroll brother, from the clan of overlords at Leap Castle, Tipperary, took out his sword and pierced his O'Bannon heart with one thrust, and his blood poured all over the chapel's holy altar."

The nun covered her mouth. "Oh, may St. Julian preserve us! What a foul act!"

"Not so foul," I smiled at her. "My many O'Bannon brothers rebelled, and when they opened the door to a hidden dungeon, in 1900, they found hundreds of human skeletons, and most of them were named O'Carroll. Since that priestly O'Bannon's death started it all, he was rewarded by God with a lucky re-birth inside me, these many hundreds of years later. My mother said my piercing scream, when I was born, cracked both of the doctor's eyeglasses. I suppose I forgot to yell, when that O'Carroll bastard ran me through, back in 1532!"

Was it my fear that I would not be able to stop my sister from killing herself making me feel this way? Or, was God attempting to get my attention, one last time, before allowing me to finally escape the pain of not communicating with Him anymore?

"Father O'Bannon, is it then?" I realized I was now following a very large man, a man whose swagger reminded me of my father Grady before he was lost to the war. The same bulging biceps, the identical glance backward and flick of his sausage fingers, simultaneously bid me come forward and yet keep me in my subservient place. He was, indeed, a paradigm of testosterone-driven energy and paradoxical movements.

"Yes. That's the name. Don't wear it out," I blurted, realizing, too late, that I was tugging on Superman's cape.

The big man in front just shook his bald head and laughed. "Always with the gallows humor, hey Father?" After two-hundred-seventy-eight steps, we were at the end of the long hallway, having passed continuous gray rooms with locked gray doors. Each door had a seven-by-eight-inch wire mesh window, giving one a glimpse, if one so desired, into the insanity that dwelled within.

"Here we are." The burly man opened the door and motioned for me to step inside. "Did I ever tell you, Father? Over the years at St. Anne's, we've had two former bishops, four monsignors, three priests, and seven nuns. And now, your sister, and her roommate. One side of the ward is for the men. One is for the women. Never the twain shall meet, as they say. Each patient must be restrained, however, as they become violent without such restraint."

I had seen such restraints on a human only once before. A patient on the first floor of St. Anne's suddenly began waving his arms, and then his arms became punchers of two fists, and he ended his stay on the first floor by punching me in the face. The twisted gray jacket they wound around his torso and then linked behind his back with a chain was now on Rose and her companion on the other bed.

COMMUNION

"Two to a room. Not bad, huh Rose? Right, Mother Superior?" The burly man gestured with his ham hocks waving toward the two women, who were leaning back on big pillows, on the two beds. If not for the straight-jackets, they might have been mistaken for two cloistered nuns, forbidden to speak by vows of silence. As usual, their arms were restrained, under the top coverlet, by what I had once heard called "the Arms of Jesus," by a delusional, pregnant nun. That deluded nun, after giving unholy birth, was once a Mother Superior on the first floor. She was now staring into space in front of me. Her lips moved silently, in rhythm with some insane prayer or curse coming from within.

"If you get a word out of either one of these women, I want to know about it, Father. Never heard a peep. For two years. They never speak, no matter what. But they can still use their nails and teeth, by God!" The burly man held out his two muscular forearms. They were indented with tooth puncture scars, and jagged-pale scratch lines, interwoven with the man's two tattoos. St. Anne's pale blue image on his left arm, and Mary, Mother of God, on his right. Quite a one-two punch.

"Rose is my favorite. She looks out at the spirit world like she's already dissolved into it. When she bites you, she's always smiling." He laughed. "We never remove the Arms of Jesus on these two."

"What is your name?" I asked him. I had never seen him in the 3,650 days I have been visiting Rose.

"Labre, Father. Benedict Joseph. French Canadian by birth. My father was a chimney sweep in Fall River, and my mother was a full-blood Mi'kmaq, from Quebec. I keep them going. They're down on the first floor now. What's your name? Never seen you up here before."

I wondered how that could be. If he kept his parents downstairs, then I must have seen him at some point during my daily visits. When he pushed me down into the green, patched armchair provided for infrequent guests, I knew I was in big trouble.

I tried to send my mind away again, to some comfortable setting in the past, possibly even to Tipperary in 1532, because this giant's hands were around my neck, and he was squeezing my

41

throat. My heart was racing, and my mind was trying to process what was happening to me. I could feel his huge thumbs digging into my carotid arteries, and I could barely breathe.

"Listen, you phony priest. I seen you get your robe from the laundry. You think I'm blind?"

I was panicked, and when he finally released his grip on my throat, I coughed and looked over at Rose. Her head was looking straightforward, and her sparkling green eyes were set upon Benedict, freezing his huge frame in her stare. The orderly wiped his sweating brow with the back of his hairy right forearm. It was the size of my thigh. He had the same rare, emerald-colored eyes as Rose and I had. On the night she went mad, Rose had taken her muumuu off, and she was naked beneath. She began to dance provocatively in front of the psychiatric ambulance team, and she then shouted, raising her fist into the air, before fainting in their arms. "Sisters! Keep the power!" I now remembered who one of the men on that team was. He was Benedict Joseph Labre. He didn't recognize me. However, as he stared at me, his green eyes boring into me, the final Truth began to appear in my memory, like a visit to Hades.

In the months and years following her commitment, I began finding myself taking risks also. I ran nude at three in the morning, before Mass, outside the rectory, and along the forest path next to the Lizzie Borden Museum. I shouted into the dewy air as I ran, piercing the early morning darkness, holding my black robe and underwear, carefully draped over my right forearm. like a reptile's shed skin. You see, I was also having an intimate love affair with the rectory's housemaid, Kathleen O'Rourke. Kate had, one night, when Rose was out with her beau, Tony, shared a secret with me. "My mother went mad and killed herself in front of me." I took her into my arms, cradled her shoulders and heaving breasts against my chest, and we made sinful, passionate love all that night, and into the next day.

This traumatized, red-haired maid and I had this single gruesome fact in common, and it was enough for my tortured mind to reconcile it to God, as I then knew Him. However, at that same moment of intercourse, I also knew I had broken my sacred vows of chastity and obedience. I knew my crooked path was bending toward perdition. At first, I tried praying longer, and with more zeal. I knelt in rice, I staggered around in the darkness, whipping my bare back and buttocks with a cat-o-nine-tails I had procured from the little shop inside the French-Canadian museum. The slowly disappearing lifeblood of my soul was dripping from my eyes, blinding me, for an eternity. So, I ran nude with my lover, along the path toward the wilderness, and our hearts beat faster with collective fear, and our carnality lit the embers of Lucifer's domain.

I had brought all of this tortured reality into this room, on this chilly fall day, with these two mute women, one of whom is my twin sister. Could the irony be more tangible? It hung, thick in the air around them, like the white-hot nucleus of a lunatic's dream.

When my mind finally began to dissolve into the abyss, I again looked over at Rose. Her black hair was cut short, for safety, and when her head turned toward me, I became transfixed by an inner vision from our past. When she spoke the following words, my memory began to disappear, and hers began to awaken.

"Anthony? Where have you been all this time?" Rose said.

***

I am the missing cog in this crazy little mystery wheel. Name's Benedict Joseph Labre. I was outside when I saw the kid come out the back door of the whore house. It's my job to spot any possible new converts for the Sister's cause. She pays me ten times what St. Anne's used to pay me. When she had her miraculous recovery, in 1972, I was there. I was also there, ten years earlier when we picked her and her brother up at that run-down apartment next door to the Lizzie Borden Bed and Breakfast Museum on Second Avenue.

When I seen the kid reach down into the gutter and pick up one of our flyers, I decided to talk to him. The kid had no memory, except for a voice he told me he kept on hearing inside his head. This voice always said the same thing, "Sisters! Keep the Power!" I thought maybe Sister O'Bannon might cure him, and he wouldn't need to search for his history any longer. He knew his age, and it was ten. He was so small and skinny he looked five.

As we entered the tent at the end of Mill Road, we heard shouts of "hallelujah" and "praise God" erupting from different wooden folding seats, with people in them, scattered all around on the earthy loam of the revival meeting. At the back of the tent, Sister O'Bannon stood erect upon the wooden riser. She wore a brilliant, white silk robe, and her black hair was long and curly. The platform was just wide enough for her to take six steps in any direction, like a sundial's pointer. Sister O'Bannon was ready to meet the next candidate for her healing touch, and she motioned to me. I was standing with the kid near the winding steps that led up to her.

"Benedict. Bring him to me." Her voice was clear and commanding, just the way it was when she came out of her psychotic trance on the second-floor violent ward the year before.

With the ten-year-old boy in my arms, I walked up the winding ramp. A voice from somewhere in the audience began to chant, "Sisters! Keep the power!" Soon, hundreds of the people, assembled there in the shadows, were taking up the same refrain, over and over again. After I set the boy down, about ten steps from her, I raised my arms above my bald head and shouted along with the audience, "Sisters! Keep the power!"

Sister O'Bannon locked her green eyes upon the boy, as his thin body and shaking legs stumbled toward her. Rose understood what must happen now because she was no longer in a trance, so she stepped toward the boy, with the utmost care, as if she were Eve, and this was their return to the innocence of Paradise. She stopped before him, reflecting her green eyes with his green eyes, before making her move, stepping into *his* space, taking *his* hand, infusing *him* with a vision that would last forever in his mind.

The green eyes of Sister O'Bannon searched the green eyes of the boy, her son, and she placed both hands on the top of his head, while still staring at him. When her son smiled up at her, she asked, to be certain, "What is your name?"

"I think it's O'Bannon," he told her, and she began to cry. She had, at that very moment, remembered giving him birth. The

Church had never told her about this birth because it was a sin. I think it's another miracle when she remembered having her boy.

The wise man said, "You do not seek out the Truth. The Truth finds you." The boy saw the Truth, as Sister O'Bannon touched her son's head, and I explained to him what had happened when he was born. I was there inside St. Anne's, working as an orderly. "When you was born, your identity disappeared, because the Archdiocese always gives bastards away to adoption agencies. You got sold by one of the poorest Catholic agencies in Fall River. They give you to some businesswoman who ran a whore house with a tavern downstairs. You never seen your ma again until today."

I now want to explain what happened that night when she became pregnant. Now that Sister Rose can remember, she will do the honors for us. Afterward, I will turn over the diary I found in her brother's possession when he exchanged places with her, on the violent ward, on that night one year ago today. She spoke to the entire audience, with a loud and clear voice, and we all listened in complete rapture.

"Before I went completely insane, on that rainy night of October 22, 1962, my brother, Jackie, grabbed my shoulders, and I immediately stopped screaming, but I lost my memory. Jackie knew the ambulance from St. Anne's would take its sweet time, as he had waited for it many times before, in his delusional reality as a priest and teacher from the rectory down the street from our apartment."

There was complete silence inside the tent. I held the boy's hand in my own, sheltering him, as I would my mother and father.

"That night, before Benedict and his team had arrived, during a howling wind and pouring rain outside, the odor of my marijuana incense grew intense inside Jackie's nostrils. My twin brother looked around our threadbare apartment next door to the Lizzie Borden Museum, and he believed he saw a halo over my head, and he told me so. Anthony, my husband, and I were living there, and we just had a big fight. Tony had called Jackie when I began acting crazy. When Jackie picked up my joint from the dresser, lit it, and inhaled, the apartment soon became, to him, his rectory. He was no longer an unemployed, alcoholic preacher, spouting scripture to the multitudes, on the streets of Fall River. He believed he was a respected Jesuit teacher, Father Jackie O'Bannon, who had given his twin sister, Rose, and her new husband, Anthony, a respite from the storm."

I knew what was coming next, and I wondered if the little boy should hear it. She was looking down at him when she spoke, so I knew her words were also meant for him.

"Anthony Nicolosi's postal carrier bag lay on its side in the corner, next to his dead body, with the letters spilling out into a fresh pool of his blood. Anthony had not gone on his route that day, as I was having a nervous breakdown, so he had called my brother, whom Tony had met, the day before, while on his delivery route downtown. Jackie had recently committed himself to the first floor, as an outpatient, of St. Anne's psychiatric ward. Jackie had told me, in one of his delusionary manic states as a priest, that Tony had been cheating on me. When I confronted him about it that night, Tony told me it was true. He was cheating on me with other women he met on his route. I can remember it now. I killed him with the butcher knife in our kitchen. My husband was dead before Jackie arrived."

I was shocked, to say the least. I knew nothing about this. That day, in 1962, according to his now newly-awakened sister, insane Father Jackie O'Bannon had smiled down at his catatonic sister, Rose, and he picked her up in his arms. She remembered he carried her into the backroom to the bed. When our ambulance crew finally arrived, he was still inside her, on the bed, and their naked bodies were sweaty, their arms gripping each other in a death-like embrace. They weren't dead, however, because I seen their green eyes had frozen stares inside separate realities. Eventually, after I pried them apart, they were both committed, into the Arms of Jesus, inside St. Anne's. Now I know that Jackie O'Bannon soon became Father Jackie, and he wandered among the patients on the first floor, inside his non-violent delusion. His fear was building inside, for those ten years, until he finally dared to go up those stairs to the violent ward, to make his holy penance with her. I was his escort.

Rose was released from St. Anne's the year before, in 1972. When she came out of her catatonia, I told her that her brother, Jackie, had stolen a priest's robe, from the first-floor laundry, to fool the staff, and she told me she thought he was a priest who had come to give her Extreme Unction.

Much later, after having passed the hospital's interview process, she was released. In 1962, she had been judged legally insane, for the murder of her husband, and the incest relationship with her brother. Jackie, I guess, believed she would be judged insane if he raped her. Ten years later, in 1972, she was judged sane, and she could begin to live again outside St. Anne's, and the Church's steely-soft grip. Those ten years inside St. Anne's were empty in her mind, but she believed what me and the hospital staff told her, and now she had miraculously remembered what had happened on that night in 1962.

Jasmine

"You do not need to leave your room. Remain sitting at your table and listen. Do not even listen, simply wait, be quiet, still and solitary. The world will freely offer itself to you to be unmasked, it has no choice, it will roll in ecstasy at your feet." — Franz Kafka

I met Professor Robert Featherstone when I taught with him at the many freeway flyer colleges we instructed, from the trunks of our cars, to make a living for over twenty-five years, as adjunct teachers in San Diego County. I would not have undertaken this story about him, as he was the writer, not I, had it not been for the email he sent me during the time we all believed was the conclusion of the Novel Coronavirus-19 Plague. We learned to gradually shorten this name, as the bodies piled up, until it was simply COVID, or even 19. As Robert phrased it, "It was when you became a good guy by wearing a mask, and the people without them were the ones we didn't trust."

I was the professor who had a Ph.D., in American Studies, but Bob was the guy with an M.A., who was both a teacher and a creative writer. For this, I admired him. It takes a lot of guts to self-publish your work, especially at the age of 74, with nobody interested in what you wrote. Bob wrote Historical Mysteries, and I had the great pleasure of reviewing every one of the books he wrote. We were both retired and hunkered-down to our lonely lives of quiet desperation, such as they were when I received Bob's email on the evening of July 17.

Dear Matthew, he began. We Boomers still use the rather antiquated salutations leftover from the bygone years of letter-writing. I suppose, technically speaking, I am not a Boomer, as I was born in 1952, and Bob was born in 1946. However, I have always revered the 1950s, as a halcyon period in our country's brief history, and Bob was a radical child chiseled out of the 1960s, which made us intellectual adversaries on many topics, including the one topic about which Bob began his letter: Advaita Vedanta and Reincarnation.

My friend, I have finally met the woman of my dreams. Her name is Aahana Archarya. She is a poor single woman, and teacher from the Brahman caste, living in northern India, near the second most sacred river, the Yamuna. I looked up her first name right away. It means to exist. Can that be more coincidental? You know my second great love is the Existentialists—Albert Camus and Franz Kafka, specifically. I call her my "Sky Princess," and I am deeply in love for the first time since Sarah died. You remember how the only big fight before Sarah and I got married was about the fact that she wasn't a writer? My Hindu love princess, however, is a real poet! Can you believe it? She calls herself a Shiva religious seeker. She is a bit young, 42, but after I taught her how to write with her senses, she fell in love with me! She translates her poetry with Google, and I fix her English errors and give her suggestions about poetic techniques. She dedicates her work to me online! She tells me the most intimate details of her life in India, about her loss of money, everything. I have made her appreciate her artistic talents, and I am helping her start an online school to replace the one she lost when both her parents died, five years ago.

I was suspecting the worst after he mentioned financially helping her. Robert is a fine man, but his one Achilles heel is that he gives away his money to any philanthropic cause that tugs at his heartstrings. The Syrian refugees, the homeless, nurses fighting COVID, or the Advaita Vedanta Center. A new cause would pop up each year we were in retirement. He was wrong about his fight with Sarah as well. The biggest fights he had with her were over his self-publishing business and his so-called "philanthropy." When he began telling me more about this woman, this Aahana, I began to worry about where this relationship had been going for the past four months.

He told me he saw her photo for the first time after many meetings on Facebook. She was dark, no surprise there, as most Indians are dark. But after what he knew about her activities and (most especially) after reading some of her translated poetry, he believed he could see past her body and into her heart and soul. He told me she had the stare of someone who knew what real beauty was but was often misunderstood by others, so her dark eyes were quite wary as if she expected the observer might run away with her heart, and never return it. Perhaps they might keep it for ransom. Her cheeks and pronounced, Asiatic jawbones made her appear to have stuffed some prized nuts, or maybe family gems, inside them. He said she was too infatuated with her prizes to give them up so easily. She would fight you if you tried to take them, and it came at you through her stare of beautiful mistrust. She was a seeker after impermanent joy and wanted a brief respite of calm in a world that, to her, was breaking down all around her. Miss Aahana Archarya was a teacher without students, a woman adrift in a sea of despair. And yet, he believed in her love. He believed he could make her into a seeker of poetic Truth.

***

I must take a break at this point. You see, Robert just informed me in this letter that he's traveling to India to ask this woman for her hand in marriage. There are still most of the COVID safety measures in place, and it is this pasted information that he included at the bottom of his email that is most worrisome: "Yamuna River. Hindu mythology includes a special mention of this river. According to the legend, the source of the Yamuna River is a glacial lake known as Saptarishi Kund, where there is a temple dedicated to the Goddess Yamuna, sister of Yama, the God of Death. That is why people who take a bath in the holy waters of the river get rid of the fear of death."

Yes, he underlined that last sentence, and this is what was troubling. In point of fact (I'm using an expression Robert often uses in his mysteries), I will allow Robert to take over the narrative from this point forward. I am in no emotional condition to do so. We shared many things, including my "coming out" at age 54 as a homosexual, and the fact that I had a morbid fear of death. As it so happens, so did Robert.

***

*D*ear Matthew,
    You can't believe how different it is in India. It is so much a clash of cultures that I, as a creative writer, am dumbfounded. It is no wonder Aahana didn't attempt to describe her land to me over Facebook Messenger. I would assume she could only write about it in purely poetic terms, in Sanskrit, because mere language—whichever one--could never contain the sensory bombardment that greets one while traveling upon the streets heading to her city in the north. Agra is about 8,179 miles by hot air balloon from San Diego. Of course, I took a jet. It was like being together with a collection of masked desperados. We had two seats between us, and the flight attendants wore Air India embossed masks. I had some chickpeas with masala sauce, as this is what I eat at home. I can microwave the packages I buy from Costco.

    I landed at Indira Gandhi International in Delhi. I was told it would be three and a half hours drive down the Taj Express Highway, so I rented a car. They also said that late July was still very hot, and it would probably be over 40 degrees Celsius, or 104 in my Fahrenheit terms. I took the paper out I printed with her address: Aahana Archarya, Old Sharma Khera Road, Jasmine School House, n/45. Shamsabad, Agra. My dreams of her took over from there. Matthew, you can't believe how I looked forward to this surprise. We messaged on Facebook all that previous week. I was helping her learn how to add a sensory experience to her poetry, and we had completed that one poem "Jasmine" I forwarded to you. You know, the one on Google Docs? I kept reciting each line as I drove, smiling to myself at all the Indians still wearing masks. In my country, the good old USA, we had riots, murders, and protests about wearing masks inside stores, much less driving down freeways. One Texas congressman had even said it was every citizen's "patriotic duty" to risk COVID infection for the good of the economy. In India, with deaths reported in the single thousands, they seem to have taken the risk much more seriously.

I'M GOIN' DOWN

No karaoke sing-along to the radio for me, old friend. I had memorized the entire poem, and her beautiful face comes into my vision as I recite:

We met.
We have known each other for centuries.
You're a mature lover, and I'm an immature lover.
The way you fill me when we embrace; can anyone give me such bliss?
Yes, a beloved, and the one who rules my heart.
Jasmine is my loving heart.

I helped her understand that the refrain 'Jasmine is my loving heart' would add to the underlying pathos of the piece. She had difficulty understanding sensory poetry, although I knew she was a natural. I told her about the difference between William Wordsworth and William Blake, and how Blake (my favorite) did not romanticize his poems the way Wordsworth did. She needed a 'Tyger' burning brightly in her work to make it "sing with passion." I also had a problem getting her to tell me about her past love. She is forty-two, after all, and she must have experienced some passion. She couldn't simply be the stereotypical "schoolmarm" from my cultural perspective. Her culture has so much radiance, color, and dancing mysticism. Sex positions in the 'Kama Sutra,' the thousands of years of Tantric energy, and the worship of the divine opposites in the coming together of the love act. The left-handed way of any sexual union, including using drugs to heighten the experience, and the right-handed way, the preferred method, between husband and wife. She wrote:

My loneliness is incomplete without you. With this feeling, I returned home.
But you didn't notice me.
I wanted to see and get the affection of your mother.
Nothing in this world matches the Aanchal of mother,
but you didn't feel me worthy enough to deserve her hug.

It is time for tea, and eons have passed since I had tea with you; your favorite ginger tea is ready. I am sitting on the lawn and with every sip, I can feel
you sitting in front of me.
Jasmine is my loving heart.
I can see your smile in the tea clearly; you are too close, even when you are far from me.

Matthew, you know the moment I knew she loved me as a man? It was the ending she created in the poem. All of what I just recited into my phone is what she added later. The climax came, at my suggestion, earlier. These were the words she wrote that captured my consciousness and made me come here to her:

In the morning, when the unbloomed buds smile at me, with the warmth of the sun's rays, it feels as if you are also smiling down on me. Are you fighting my love, as you fight our enemy? Please don't say you have forgotten me!
Your smile and jasmine's smile are complementary to me when you are not around,
When the blooming flowers are kissed, the petals give me a sensation of your lips. They are not your lips, but I still try to kiss them repeatedly.
When I touch them with my hands, the velvety feeling gives me the caress of your palms,
when I am close to you.
Jasmine is my loving heart.
I adorn my hair by making them into a garland, wound inside the lattice of my family's wood gazebo. When the blossoms squish, and my ears are close, they whisper something to me, as you would do.
Sometimes, when I take them up into my hands, filling my palms with the petals, I can embrace you.
Whenever I feel lonely, your love is replaced by them. I'm quiet. Their touch indulges me by momentarily giving me

53

*your gentle caress upon my cheek, or my forehead, or my
bare legs, after my bath.*

This touch makes every part of me happy.

Jasmine is my loving heart.

*I see the child-like you in these flowers; they play with me as
you used to. I dance in the springtime fields, and cast these
hearty blooms around me like you cast away the enemy with
your sword.*

Whenever I see their yellow softness,

*I see the reflection on your face. We are bound together in
their fragrance; you and I, forever together.*

*We are bound to each other until you return, and we can
marry.*

*You have not returned. Each moment now becomes misery.
I surge through the day, pushing things over, muttering
curses under my breath. My father believes I am mad, so he
buys me a puppy, with a small black diamond in the middle
of his narrow forehead.*

*I take my puppy to the fields of jasmine. I hope I can
recapture our love. The wind is strong against my dress, and
it billows up, the puppy whines at my yellow slippers.*

*I pick him up, and his eyes are red-rimmed, his tiny head
downcast as if he knows the truth.*

*He is dying. I place him down within the fragrant blossoms,
my jasmine. My heart beats furiously inside my breast.*

*My brother runs up to me from the village. "He has been
slain, sister. His body is being cremated at the river by his
family. Will you go?"*

*I cannot go. My puppy is dying, and I pick him up. A few
stray flowers are also in my arms with his warm body.*

The sun has gone down, and it is night.

*I hold the tiny pup in my arms, the flowers enfolding him, but
I can hear his last gasps of painful suffering against me. The
yellow moon is full, radiant, glowing down upon my
upturned face. My love, where have you gone? My world has
changed forever.*

The puppy's tiny teeth rip into my hand before he succumbs.

Jasmine is my loving heart.

I added the part about the puppy's teeth biting her. I told her I got it from J. D. Salinger. He was talking about a widower who attained enlightenment while gazing at the full moon. He, however, had been allowing his cat to pierce his hand's flesh. What's the difference? Cat. Dog. It's all fair between artists, right? She told me she loved that detail, and that's when I knew she loved me, not as a 74-year-old father, but as a lover. I will show her the website I've created for her new online school, and then I'll ask for her hand. Remember how I told you about the four puppies she saved from the road, birthed by the 'street bitch,' as she called her? That's why I added the puppy into her poem. I thought it would get to her, and she would love me for it. It worked!

***

*M*atthew, as I pull into the dirt road leading to her schoolhouse, I can't avoid comparing the recent demonstrations back home against racist police brutality with my demonstrations in the late Sixties and early Seventies. Today, the demonstrations are sparked by the death of George Floyd, an unemployed security guard, by the Minneapolis policeman who had been reprimanded eighteen times previously for his actions against citizens.

You know, of course, that I was with the Vietnam Veterans Against the War back in 1972, when I marched with Ron Kovic from the state university in Fullerton, over to the Honeywell Chemical building across the road from the campus. Ron gave us a speech about our government creating the napalm that was dropped from helicopters onto civilians, and there was that iconic photo by an independent journalist, of a girl running naked down a dirt road, just like the one I'm now on, her body burned by the jellied flame. This was the cruel invention of horror we demonstrated against. Not the murder of a fellow American. The murder of people thousands of miles away. How times change. Right? My compatriots in time, these demonstrators, are laying down in the road, in dying postures, to reflect Mr. Floyd's last moments, as the cop had his knee on the poor black man's thorax. "I can't breathe." And, "Momma! Help me!" These words echoed in my mind along with our refrains of 'Peace now!' And, 'We don't want your fucking war!' It seems as if the Fascists we screamed about have finally come home to roost. Hey, old buddy?

You know, Matthew, we've talked about these changes in our own culture many times. So have Aashana and I. In Advaita Vedanta, the very process of change is seen as one of the realities of suffering in Samsara. For example, these kids today can't even locate the corporations responsible for our weapons of mass destruction. The policies have been purposely convoluted since 1972 when we could uncover the guilty corporations creating such illegal carnage in our name. Today? Not so much. The Supreme Court says corporations are now "people," and the masses aren't even blinking an eye to demonstrate about that. Nor, are the corporate tax give-aways being demonstrated against, except for the brief but unheralded Occupy Wall Street fiasco. No, one of my main personal gripes, the Private Equity Firms, under whose control thousands of nursing home residents have died because of the cut-backs these firms made to lower labor costs. Then they terminate critical nursing jobs and provide few and inadequate medical devices, and then there's the cruel warehousing of our poor disabled elderly inside these torture homes. These corporations euphemistically call them "Heaven's Glen," or "Mother's Best Choice." And, of course, there are the hundreds of thousands of jobs being lost when these private firms "occupy and take over" publicly-held companies, like Toys-R-Us. Nope. No street demonstrations anymore for that stuff. You and I, as old Leftists, know those practices are the real, underlying cause of the poverty for everybody in our poor neighborhoods, no matter the racial mixture, and that the police are just protecting the interests of those fat cats living in the rich neighborhoods.

I digress. I'm coming up to her house now. I should be thankful I can drive at 74, I suppose. Not having enough gratitude is one of my character defects, as you and I well know. This town of Shamsabad has only 33,000 people in it. That's small for India. It has lush vegetation, however, and it has the tourist attraction of the Taj Mahal, which is north about 800 miles, but tourists also make it down here. Ironically, the Taj Mahal was a mausoleum built by a Muslim King for his wife in the Seventeenth Century occupation of these parts. They also have a tourist attraction that looks strangely like the Eiffel Tower in Paris. Oh well. They attract over seven million folks a year.

In San Diego, we have the zoo and the wild animal park, and, of course, my least favorite, the Comicon festival of SciFi freaks. I guess they sell some doo-dads and stuff to help the local merchants. And the restaurants need some help after the lock-downs. Everybody here is still wearing masks, however. And they're Hindu women, not Muslim. Aahana doesn't care for the Muslims much. They put poison in the bananas that the elephants eat. A pregnant female elephant recently died in the Yamuna River. She watched it all on her cell phone. She has no TV. Never watches movies—even Bollywood romances. She hates romances. That's why I'm here, right, old friend? Bring romance into this poor woman's life at last!

You know Sarah would love it here. She was the world traveler, not I. After Vietnam, you know the story. I went back to graduate school, demonstrated, and vowed to never travel outside the United States again. From what I've read, the vets these days are offing themselves more than our group did back in the day. I suppose it might be because of the video game recruiters they have today. Kids think they're going into some giant first-person shooter game. What a let-down! Old Oliver Stone, Ronnie Kovic and I knew exactly what we were getting ourselves into. My dad was a Pearl Harbor Survivor, and I had to go, right? These days, the poor kids and fundamentalist Christians from the farms get recruited the most. And, the ones who are natural-born killers, like in Stone's movie.

Wait. What's that big crowd of citizens up there? That's where Aahana's schoolhouse is supposed to be, according to my Google maps GPS. There's even this TV camera van, with Hindi writing on the side of it. All these Hindus standing around in masks, peering into the building. I have to get out now, but I'll leave it on record. I feel like a reporter myself. This is kind of exciting, isn't it?

***

*M*atthew, old pal, I can see the beginning of the new school *she told me about. I've never seen her in person. Even over the cell phone. Just videos she showed me of her traipsing about all over India, going to one Hindu temple after another, searching for God. She was building this school for the poor kids she taught. I told her I could save her with the online school I'm creating. I don't know. I don't have much money. Bill Gates isn't going to pitch in. He's too busy with his disease causes. I suppose a big part of me is like my father, the old horn dog. I just want to get her into the sack. Maybe it could work, you know? But these steel rods look kind of ominous sticking out of the bricks and cement up into the air, like omens of doom. I told her about the poem by Shelley, 'Ozymandias.' She liked it.*

Hey, maybe these people are here because they heard I was working on her new online school. We're calling it the Jasmine Spirit Online School. These people are standing six feet apart. Not like the beaches back home Insane Diego. These people understand diseases. I've always thought Aahana was too scientifically inclined in her poetry. She never takes risks, like Sylvia Plath or Anne Sexton. When I pasted her 'Lady Lazarus,' she gave me one of those surprise emojis.

'What's going on here, folks? Does anybody speak English? Is this where the school principal, Aahana Archarya, lives?'

A few of the women are staring at me with daggers. Then, this dark-skinned lady, in a mask, and a wide-body and huge gold sari, frowns and points inside. Her caterpillar brows almost engulf the gold Bindi between them. "She there. With Constable Prabhakar."

Did you hear her, Matthew? I'm going to shut this off for now. I don't like the looks of what might be going on. I'll tell you what happens later.

***

I t's me. Matthew, alias Deus ex Machina. I never did hear back from Robert. I recorded this. I was able to piece together what happened from the newspaper and television stories. I'll be honest with you. You aren't going to like what I am about to tell you. It doesn't exactly fit with a Bollywood or even a Hollywood ending. Reality never does, does it?

The town of Shamsabad was evicting the former school principal, Aahama Archarya, for non-payment of her rent, but also for her seductive poetry on the Internet, discovered by a hacker at the Vardhaman College of Engineering, while he was snooping around in her Google Doc files. He showed it to his mother, the town gossip. And, one thing led to another, and the tongues began to wag. Aahama had told her cousin about the wealthy American who had become smitten by her, but she saw him as a father figure. Both her parents, so said the news reports, had died, and this led to her family's fight over the school and the property. It seems Aahama had been swindled by a few of her relatives, so she was, like Robert, down to her poetry, the vacant lot upon which the start of her school was standing, and the rent she paid the city to reside in the old school's building.

The news reports said they drove up to the end of the Yamuna, in Agra. What took place before they entered the Saptarishi Kund Lake is anybody's guess. They did find there were large rocks inside Bob's Levi pockets and in Aahana's sari. I, unlike Bob, am not a romantic at heart. I was never married. I never liked to travel, although I did twice. Once I went to a Spanish language course in Oaxaca, Mexico, and I still don't know how to speak Spanish. The second time to Puerto Rico to my niece's wedding. However, because of what's happened to Bob, my only real friend,

I am now going to attempt to make good on something I told him I had never done. I told them that although I was gay inside, I had never experienced sexual relations with a man. I was too afraid. That's what the reporters said about Aahana. She never married, and yet she was always accused by the women in Samshabad of being a temptress and a slut. I am going out to become a slut, for once in my life.

And, as for my best friend, Professor Robert Featherstone, I made up my fiction about his demise. I believe he confessed to Aahana Archarya about his war experience. He was part of a platoon that burned an entire village and killed all the animals. I believe he told her about Sylvia Plath, and about Anne Sexton, and, most especially, about Virginia Woolf. He told her they should go out into the pristine, cool waters of Saptarishi Kund, as it was purified of the garbage and drifting offal that usually polluted it, or so the newspapers said. The young reporter wondered why they would commit suicide when things had cleaned up for once. He was young. He did not understand. They had won the magical promise of that lake. They no longer feared death, and they were artists, in love, in a world that abhorred romantic love between desperate characters.

Bob was very desperate. Aahana, I would imagine, by the looks of the final stanzas of her "Jasmine" poem, was also reaching her limits. However, they had their time together, for four months, sharing their poem, writing it together, falling in love, each in his or her way, 8,000 miles apart. Isn't this the nature of our New Age, post-COVID? Coming together yet fearing to be close. Not yet understanding that it is not only race that separates us, but money. And it is not fear that prevents us from taking the plunge but losing our fear of being desperate.

They were cremated together out in the Yamuna River. Nobody came, including me. Aahana Archarya was a disgrace to her town. And Bob Featherstone? Just another crazy former hippie vet that used to go there to buy ganja and stay stoned during their variety of festivals to Shiva or some other Hindu god.

I do have something to leave you with, besides the tears I have shed for my best friend of all these years. Aahana worked on their poem, alone, in the silence of the third floor of her schoolhouse.

Bob never got the chance to correct her grammar, but I thought it was good enough to let you read it. It may enlighten you. Who knows? Stranger things have happened in this world of ours.

> *I still remember your habit of swimming in that in the pool after tea to get refreshed this summer,*
> *today I am sitting near the same pool in my house in which you once enjoyed swimming and today I have specially decorated this pond, I love your fragrance.*
> *What a wonderful match with the mix of Bella bark and sandalwood fragrance in which you were ecstatic and enjoy swimming for hours and I sat on the shore watching you enjoy this bliss,*
> *Today I am searching in this empty pond in your absence. I put my feet under the water ripples hit my feet with the weave--like you used to drag me while swimming,*
> *Today, I felt so happy that I also jumped into the water to get you, filled my arms as you used to drag me into the floating water,*
> *And I believe this moment to be true for many hours holding in arms around you with every breath.*
> *I have learned to live losing myself in memories of you; these are the ones that inspire me to live every second.*

It is I once more, Matthew Levine, with this addendum. I *will* go out tonight. I will put baby powder under the arms of my pudgy, aged body, and look far enough beyond my fears, so I can finally get laid in Hillcrest, the gay community of San Diego. Fuck it, as Bob would say. Fuck it.

But I am standing here, staring at the door to my condo, talking into my fucking cell phone, as if I can still talk to Bob. I am wishing I had Bob's fearlessness. I am wishing I was the writer, the way he was. I am wishing I had fought for something, other than for my survival. I am touching the doorknob, but I think about COVID. I fear death. I think about Bob and Aahana. I turn around, and I walk back inside.

I'm Goin' Down

My sponsor, an old chopper pilot from the Dink Wars, told me to take this gig. We are a gig economy now, right? Want a trained and efficient sniper to take out anybody on the face of the planet? Got it. Want fifteen zombies to suffocate and separate a journalist who is bad-mouthing your regime? Have to do the job inside a foreign embassy? No problem. Got it. Want to save folks from pulling the plug, pillow therapy, shotgun mouthwash, splodeydope, Allah oops, copicide, or celebricide? Got it. No, I got it. I got that job. Gunny says I can stay clean and sober this way. He says I'm too educated to exit on the Eagle's tailpipe. I care too much about my Eagle shit payments and my education bennies to do that. When the phone rings, I am here. San Diego Veteran Suicide Prevention Hotline. J. C. Spencer, Hospital Corpsman First Class, USN, retired, at your service.

"Hey, Spence. You still hanging out at that Guru's house?"

Curly O'Brien, the bald, dimpled-face jarhead to my left, in the center cubicle, is addressing me. He's paralyzed from the waist down, due to an errant IED in the early days of the Fight for Saddam's Asshole in 2002. Otherwise known as the Iraq Green Zone, located in beautiful downtown Baghdad; he was blown up on the road to the airport. I guess that's why he's on the Eagle Shits Suicide watch with me.

As we used to say in the Zone, "IEDs will set you free!" But, as we're both released monsters from the Corps (although I still say the Navy "hooyah" and not the jarhead's "oorah"), we have the same Charlie Foxtrot attitude toward civilian life. As my sponsor tells me, over and over, it seems, "J. C. are our Lord's initials, Spencer. You don't deserve 'em. I picked you up off the grass in Balboa Park, sucking on a crack pipe. You're no fucking martyr to our country, you idiot. You're an addict, just like me. It's harder to hit a speeding target, so I'm making you stay busy, Doc. Get it?"

I got it. But that doesn't mean I can't improve my spiritual well-being. I mean, you can get only so much spiritual advice from a sixty-five-year-old, lard-ass Marine Corps enlisted Huey pilot from Oklahoma City, right?

"That's an affirmative, Curls and Whirls. My guru works at the Upas Street Vedanta Center. I'm a novice, but I think I'm getting a handle on the whole thing. You should try it. It will clean your inner clock, man, believe me."

"Oh. Yeah, right. You did tell me. He works on the head-up-your-ass street. Religion's the opiate of the people, man. Did you ever read that in one of your books, pal?"

"Hey, don't knock it, hairy triangle, until you've tried it. I've even been to the Ramakrishna Monastery to hear the Swami from New York City speak. That's where I got on the path, man. My outlook changed completely after I heard him speak."

"Roger that. Let's hear that outlook, lookout. 'Cause your phone just lit up." Curly pointed to the small red bulb at the end of my desk inside the center. We all had them. I told everyone at lunch one day that it was the Satanic equivalent to the green light from Daisy Buchanan's dock in *The Great Gatsby*. These Eagle Shit Packers didn't understand a word of what I was saying. Figures. They're all about as literate as moon dust inside a DFAC in Kandahar.

"Hello. This is the hotline. May I help you?" We were all told to K.I.S.S. it with our responses. People who want to off themselves are usually in a pretty big hurry. They don't like to beat around the bush much.

My dad was a vet, too. The gentle voice said. Her tone was so gentle that I had the strange premonition I was talking to an angel, or an alien, a far more intelligent being.

"Oh, yeah? Where'd he serve?" I asked, knowing she would get to the reason she was calling in her own sweetly feminine time.

He was at Fallujah. He told me the Italian documentary crew interviewed him. He was lobbing whiskey pete grenades at the buildings at the time. That's when he first realized the atrocities he was unwittingly committing. The Italian woman told him he was using napalm on civilians. Just like the grunts did in the jungles of Vietnam.

"Yup. Been there, done that. I was a corpsman attached to forward units in Kandahar during Operation Rhino, 2001, and later, during the fall of Baghdad. Got wounded in Rhino, they patched me up, and I was plunked down with my unit inside Iraq. That's where I met atheist numb-nuts over here, Curly O'Brien. Now I'm a Vedanta sannyasin attached to cosmic spiritual units in San Diego." I chuckled at my levity. Bad habit I have. When my wife left me to my drugs and booze, I was full of witty one-liners. That's what you got when you were an English major in college. A college drop-out. Either witty one-liners, or a job in the Marine Corps, after the Trade Center got downloaded.

Well, I'm attached to a rail on the Coronado Bay Bridge. Looking down into those far-away waves, I'd say I am pretty close to eternal spiritual rest myself. It looks so deep and gentle right now. I can almost feel the pull from up here. The wind is blowing my hair. I could be in one of those cool, slow-motion, Patine-Eternal hair commercials that I just love.

My brain was doing flip-flops. This was something I was never expecting. A kid, a girl, on the hotline? We were supposed to get vets. Wet-behind-the-ears, football-loving grunts, who were wondering why they lived and others didn't. Sitting there, with their cool Glock resting peacefully against the skull, waiting for some divine intervention coming from another asshole on the other end. My record isn't great, so far, at this. I've lost three this month already. But *this*? This was unprecedented.

"How'd you get this number, kid? This is for vets only. I think. Wait a minute. Hey, Curly. Can we take calls from the kids of vets?" I listened. Curly grunted an affirmative, high-toned grunt, which I knew meant yes. "Okay, you got me. I'm allowed to talk to you. You've just won the kid's special of the day. Fifteen minutes of hair-raising and jocular moments with J. C. Spencer, United States Navy Corpsman. I used to have a drug cabinet filled to choke a horse. Believe me. I made Trump's Surgeon General look like the dope supplier to *Sesame Street*. My initials stand for Juicer and Crack-head. I am a recovered druggie. By the way, are you high right now, little lady? Not high up, silly. I mean, high on a drug of some kind. Also, how old are you, sweetheart? You sound like fifteen going on seventy-five."

No. I don't do drugs. My dad was into that crap. I also never say shit. The Nazis said it, and I will never repeat a word that Nazis ever uttered. I am so joyful right now I might as well say what Seymour Glass said in 'Perfect Day for Bananafish.'

"You've read Salinger? What a trip you are, my young caller. You may just win the lightning round! If you climb down off that railing, that is. I was a college English major. It's your lucky day. I know Salinger. The fellow vet that he was. He was humping *The Catcher in the Rye* on D-Day. I suppose you know that, right?"

We're instructed to keep them talking. This was my attempt to make her confront the karmic music of her actions. It was a lifeline. Just a lifeline thrown to her during her present predicament. Most vets never take the toss. They were young gamers raised on what my Swami calls "dualistic reality." Good and evil. Enemy and friend. Heaven and Hell. Life and death. Bullshit and manna.

Of course. I've read all the vet authors, from Bitter Bierce to Kurt V. And, I'm sixteen. I've never been online, and I read books you can hold, smell, make notes in, and study. Just like my dad taught me. If a tree can give its life for a good book, then it must be a serious sacrifice. Dad's was a sacrifice off this same bridge. I'm looking down right now, J. C., and I can see him down inside those deep waters. He's calling me down to him.

Holy crap! She *was* going to jump! The one female who was better read than I was, and she wanted to be fish bait. At sixteen? Not on my watch, if I could help it.

"What's your name, honey? You sound so intelligent. I want to discuss literature with you some more. Can you just get down off that railing, so we can talk?"

You know, these admirals, or tourists, or whatever they are? They just keep driving past me. Everybody thinks they know where they're going so fast and so sure. Zipping off to who knows where. Moons, planets, new galaxies? I've heard all of that nonsense. When the time is right, and you're filled with the joy of the universe, then you can leave everything behind. Just like Billie says, right? Better hurry, 'cause I'm leavin' soon.

"So? Here I am, bitch! The goddamned cavalry."

Oh, guru. Where are you now? Can I get one outside call? Outside Mayaville? Those vets I lost were already Jimi Hendrixed on life. They had tombstones in their eyes, man. This kid is sixteen, and she is more tuned into the karmic afterlife than I am at thirty-eight. How can I begin to lock horns with her?

"Please. I have never been more serious. I want to know how you got so happy. What was it? Your dad? Was he into spiritual stuff, my darling? Me too! I am studying under a guru right now at the San Diego Vedanta Society. Get down, so we can talk about it."

Then, I assume you've read, at least, the Gita. My given name is Ruth. Like the Moabite woman the Jews took into their tribe because she was so cool. My father was a Jew, but my mother was from India. Krishna was trying to get it all into the poor Prince Arjuna's very thick skull. Right? When you're doing the work of the Gods, you never die. When Arjuna picked up his weapon to fight his brothers, he was not going to risk spiritual death. Nobody ever dies. Once Seymour was enlightened, he shot himself inside his Miami Beach motel room. The last thing he left was a note about a little girl he watched on a flight as she was turning her doll's head toward him. I am that Ruthie doll that looked at him. I do not play with humans anymore.

My guru told me about these kinds of humans once. Old Souls. They were born with so many previous lives that they had spiritual wisdom bursting inside them. Like Sri Ramakrishna. He was so holy and advanced spiritually that he once passed out from sheer joy when somebody closed an umbrella near him. How in the hell was I going to stop this little princess from taking what she saw as her big leap into Samadhi?

"Seymour shot himself inside his *hotel* room. He wasn't in a *motel*, little lady. See? You're not as smart as you thought you were."

I was trying one, last-ditch effort to get her locked into me. She may even be over the edge already, but I needed to try, didn't I? I was thinking hard about getting high if I did lose her. I don't know why. I never had a kid. I don't even especially *like* kids. They get all messed up on our adult fairy tales. The little princess must get her prince. Bambi's mother must get avenged. Peter Pan has to get his stories read. This was fucking life and death. Right here and right now!

He was? I could swear I read that he was in a motel. They drove to Miami, right? He and his new wife?

The hesitance in her gentle voice made me want to leap for joy. I don't know exactly why. Was it the expectation that I could save her life? No. It wasn't that. It was the possibility of keeping her spiritual being on track. I wanted to kiss Salinger for writing that story in the *New Yorker*. I didn't even care that his Estate would try to sue me for uttering its precious words over the phone. Phone? That's where they got the word "phony," right? Holden and his dead brother, Allie. Holden and his kid sister, old Phoebe. Watching her ride that Rilke Ferris Wheel at the park. That's what saved Holden's sanity! Some krout poem written in the early Twentieth Century. I wrote my one term paper about that poem in my class on Salinger. Maybe it would save Ruth. My guru always tells me that we cannot search for our destiny. It will always find us. Maybe all those suicidal vets I couldn't save were leading me to this moment. The meeting of cosmic synchronicity. Let's see. She's sixteen. When she's eighteen, I'll be forty. My mom had me when she was forty-five. Charlie Chaplin married Oona O'Neill when he was fifty-four, and she was eighteen. She was the love of Salinger's life. He never really loved any woman again. This was my chance at some kind of spiritual redemption. All those grunts who died on my watch. Under my needle. Screaming their eighteen-year-old souls into my body. Oh, Shiva. Where are you when I need you? The light force to bring us out from the night of our souls? The divine lingam, whose shards create earthly temples. Can I save my lover Shakti before she plunges into oblivion?

J. C.?

The desperation in her voice froze me.

"Yes, sweetness?" I mustered.

I must leave you all now. I'm so happy to have met you like this. It's a gift, isn't it? My mother was so sad. Back in India, the wife in the rural areas must follow her husband into death. It's called Sati. My mother did this, but she did not burn outside. She burned inside. With pills. They were both Pisces. And I am also the fishes. Our home is in the eternal ocean. Is it not?

Off the deep end. She wasn't going to do it on my watch! Fucking hell!

"Wait a minute, Ruth. I know a German poet who wasn't a Nazi. Hell, he flunked out of military school. Let me recite his poem that Salinger used in his famous book. I got an A on my paper from my professor. He was a Brahmin who was into Tantric Yoga. He published my paper for me, even though I never got to graduate. Can I recite it for you? It's the linchpin of Holden's dilemma at the end. You have read *Catcher*, haven't you, sweetheart?"

I could hear her lovely sigh of impatience. Her soul was already traveling light years ahead of my own. Was it to go down into the depths? Or, was she contemplating seriously what I just said?

Are you kidding? Of course, I've read Catcher. Mother knew Salinger was into Vedanta.

I then heard the most inspirational and magnificent sound I have ever heard. I listened, as attentively as a child on Christmas morning, as this girl climbed down from the guardrail of the Coronado Island Bridge. I held my breath, as she hummed to herself, and then she sang a few lyrics from Billie Eilish's *Listen Before I Go*. It was now my turn to seek karmic justice. Perhaps my entire spiritual fate and physical bliss were suspended in the balance of the excruciatingly long time it took for her to be ready to hear my words.

Well? I'm listening.

I wanted to suck in her breath inside that phone. I wanted to bathe in its beautifully resonant wisdom, plunge my very heart into its eternal, rhythmic beat.

"Okay. It's been a long time, but I think I still remember the words. You have to picture Holden, standing next to that carousel, in the rain, smoking. His sister, old Phoebe, is riding around and around, and he begins to cry. I said in my paper that Holden was the little guy riding the lion in this poem. His name is what that boy is doing. Holding on. He's afraid to let it all go. Karma is action, not a metaphor. But we kill for, and we are saved by metaphor. Billie understands. We're all a metaphor for something else. A symbol of hope to someone. It's what separates us from the machines in our machine age, is it not? Here we go. Here's Rilke, my dear:

Beneath a roof and with its shadow spins for just a little while the stock of painted horses—all are from the land that lingers on before it vanishes. Though some are hitched to carriages, they all show fierceness in their faces; a frightening red lion walks among them and now and then there's a white elephant. Even a stag is there, like in the woods, except he bears a saddle and above it a little blue girl, firmly fastened. And on the lion rides a boy in white, who holds on with a small hot hand; meanwhile the lion shows his teeth and tongue. And now and then there's a white elephant. And on the horses, they come passing by, girls also, luminous, almost too grown up to join this horse ride; in mid-swing they look up, somewhere, this way. And now and then there's a white elephant. And so it goes and hurries up to finish, and turns and circles only without aim. A red, a green, a gray sent gliding by, a little profile, barely seen and gone. And every now and then a smile, turned hither, enchanted, ravishing, and lavishing upon this blind and breathless game."

When I heard her crying, I knew I had hit the Diamond Sutra inside her soul. Somehow, it made up for all my years of restless nightmares, my speeding past everything in the park, my constant inability to look anyone in the eye. Her tears had sent me into Samadhi, in the here and now, and I would never forget it as long as I lived this life of boundless mystery and limitless joy.

The Jain

O n the day he became a Jain, Lance Corporal Marty Philips, on his twenty-eighth birthday, had to confront his father, Roy, about a very terrible event. After he came back from Afghanistan, Marty himself was in no great shakes. He had to get a special chit from the hospital to keep the professors at Mesa College from discussing any kind of war or violent topics in front of him. His PTSD chit was vitally important to his mental health.

The school had recently opened for classes, so they all wore masks, and the chairs were six feet apart inside small circles. However, it was this family matter that caused Marty the most stress he had ever felt, even when he was on the hills and down in the valleys of Helmand Province with the Corps.

It was his English professor, Mr. Wayland Huey, who gave him the idea to become a Jain monk. Professor Huey knew about Marty's chit, and so he was very careful about what he presented in his class. Marty supposed he wasn't the only vet in the class who might have such a "get out of mental jail free" card. They were discussing world religions, and the way they often dove-tailed into each other in mythical and mysterious ways. It was extremely fascinating to Marty, as the closest he had ever come to spiritual or religious matters was when his family had to say the "Pledge of Allegiance" before every meal and recite the "Marine Corps Hymn" before special meals, like Thanksgiving and Christmas.

Marty thought the warlords in the villages had pretty strange beliefs, but they were nothing compared to the Jains that Dr. Huey lectured about that day. As far as any kind of discipline, even the Marine Corps' idea of discipline, these Jains were far beyond any military rules or regulations. They were onto an entirely new plane of existence. As he listened to the professor explain, Marty's mind became fixated on the images it brought into his mind.

"Shvetambara monks are allowed to retain a few possessions such as a robe, an alms bowl, a whisk broom, and a *mukhavastrika*— which is a piece of cloth held over the mouth to protect against the ingestion of small insects. These objects are presented by a senior

70

monk at the time of initiation. For the non-image-worshipping Sthanakavasis and the Terapanthis, the *mukhavastrika* must be worn at all times. After initiation a monk must adhere to the great vows, called *mahavrata*s, to avoid injuring any life-form, lying, stealing, having sexual intercourse, or accepting personal possessions."

Mr. Huey pointed to the white screen, which showed a video of these Svetambara monks, walking delicately in formation, wearing their flimsy white robes, a young kid in the front of the line with a bigger version of the whisk broom, a giant peacock feather, wiping away the path of any possible living organisms that might be in the way of their journey.

Marty was thinking about the IED units he had watched sweep the roads for possible explosive devices. *Is this the same thing? Sure. Why not? One of those critters could be deadly. This kid is protecting those monks.* Marty was concerned about the sex thing, however.

"Hey, Mr. Huey?" He spoke up, and he rarely did that in any class he was in.

"Yes, Marty. Did you have a question?" Mr. Huey's wild curly-gray hair and full, gray-streaked beard were quite alien to Marty's military culture, but this monk business pressed on his consciousness like a vice. He believed it also might save him from the questions he had to ask his father later in the day.

"I just Googled this religion, and I found another sect, the Digambara, and they're in Kundalpur. They have erotic temples. There, it says, the monks and nuns carve figures of men and women having sex, and the male monks go around naked. So, do they make their money creating temple porno for the tourists? And hanging out in the nude? What's up with that?"

There was laughter throughout the class. Instead of freaking out, which was what Marty thought he would do, the professor opened his smartphone browser, raised his head, and smiled at Marty.

"What's the URL, Marty? I want to see this for myself. I don't believe I've ever heard of such a sect."

To his surprise, Marty's inquiry started a big discussion with his class members. They began to argue about the Catholic monks, who made money from their wine and brandy, and how it might compare with these Skyclad Jain monks in India. Was it hypocritical to make one's money from sexually titillating products and still maintain one's celibacy and purified moral code? How could these holy people lecture to others about human conduct?

***

On his way home from class, Marty stopped at the hardware store. He bought a mask, a whisk broom, and a ceramic bowl. The cashier, a girl with braces, was playing some "rap crap" on her phone speaker. She smiled at him and said, "Are you a beggar or an umpire?" He gave her a half-grin, told her to put a mask on, took his change, and left.

His thoughts were on what he was going to do when he confronted his father about what his two sisters had told him over Skype on a conference call earlier that day. His father was on his second marriage, and his second wife, Bernice, had two daughters from her first marriage. Roy and Bernice had two daughters, Monique and Isabel, Marty's half-sisters, who were now twelve and eighteen, and only Monique was still living at home. His two stepsisters, Barbara, age twenty-two, and Jeanene, age twenty, had moved from the house after the night in question. This was the night Marty was going to discuss with his father. Marty had not been present, as he was in-country Afghanistan at the time. But Isabel and Barbara had called him about the event, while he was in math class, just before his English class with Mr. Huey.

It was Roy's philandering ways that sent Marty's real mother, Christine, packing when Marty was eight years old. They never heard from her again. The drunken beatings and bringing hookers home had done it for her. Marty could remember only three events from that time after his mother deserted them. The first event was when he got caught cursing on his way home from Catholic school, where he was an altar boy, just after his mother left. Roy beat Marty's entire body with his belt, until his chest, back, arms and legs were black and blue. Another event was when a guy named Champ, down the street, gave Marty dog food to eat, and he laughed his ass off about it to his son, Billy, telling him what a dumb shit Marty was. Roy beat the crap out of Champ. The final event was when Roy was drunk at home, with one of his barflies, and he told Marty to tell the bitch about how babies were made. They both laughed their asses off as Marty mumbled stuff about penises and vaginas.

Bernice was an Italian from New Jersey. She'd previously been married to a used car salesman, Ed, who was arrested for armed robbery and sent to prison. When Roy and Bernice first met, in San Diego, Marty was ten years old. Roy had beaten the shit out of Bernice's former beau when the stupid wretch tried to get back with her after his prison time. Even though Ed had a Glock, Roy subdued him with a sweet taekwondo move. Bernice had divorced Ed the robber while he was locked up. After the altercation, when Ed was placed in prison again, Roy married Bernice.

Marty was confronted with a new mother, and it was all good for a while, as Roy was what they call a "periodic alcoholic." Roy, who was now fifty-two and an E-8 Master Sergeant in the Corps, was a decorated hero and had been sent to the same place Marty had been, Helmand Province, Afghanistan. But Roy had been there for four tours. Marty, who had lived with his sisters and Bernice during his father's deployments, had been there only once, for a single year. Roy had also been in Iraq for four other tours of duty.

Marty knew the media called those tours "the forever wars," and he and Roy had performed admirably, and they both were awarded a Silver Star, for Roy, and a Bronze Star for him, and Purple Hearts for both of them after being wounded in firefights. *The attacks over there were a regular occurrence*, Marty thought to himself, as he walked up to the house, a two-story affair tucked away, off the main road, in the rural town of Alpine, above San Diego. *While the Jains in India, just a few thousand kilometers from Afghanistan, practice strict non-violence, the U. S. Marines and the Taliban practice their rituals of violence with the same dedication. Pops is like his Vietnam War father, Arnie Philips. He never talks about combat.*

Today, Marty heard the same birds squawking, the same ugly jungle geranium hedges were in formation around the same

73

lone eucalyptus tree, and the same wide banner was hanging above the double doors, which read, "This is a Mask-Free Zone! Shove your masks up your asses, and salute the flag on your right as you enter. Only Corps families enter here, and they're checked every day for COVID, just like our President!"

Marty was no longer in the Corps, but he felt as if he'd been in it his entire life. He was being treated for his PTSD at the Balboa Naval Hospital after his ODMPT discharge. He was prescribed selective serotonin reuptake inhibitors. He never drank alcohol, so he didn't have to worry about mixing his drugs. He reached into his paper bag, pulled out his *mukhavastrika* and stretched it across his mouth, and pulled the elastic around his ears. Then he pulled out his broom and set it down on the deck. He stripped down to the raw, leaving his dungarees, tee-shirt, and Danner's MEB combat boots on the porch. As he stood there, he felt the warm breezes out of the canyon, and he glanced down at the state-of-the-art prosthesis for hand amputees below his right forearm, just beneath the USMC eagle, globe, and anchor tattoo.

He was one of the lucky ones that day. He lost his hand. It took a lot of programming by the technicians at Balboa, but now this myoelectric device used the signals from his body to control functions like holding the broom, which he was now doing. A few violent images flashed in his mind, but they were in slow motion, inhibited by his antidepressants, he figured.

He bent over, very slowly, delicately, and carefully, and began sweeping the ground leading up to the double-door entrance. With some satisfaction, he watched two beetles, antennae waving frantically, and a squad of ants, and they were whisked away with his broom's straw bristles, like friendly neighbors who were too drunk to get home without his help.

Plain olive-drab green nylon shorts and a polyester T-shirt were what his father always wore around the house when he was off duty. Roy was still a DI at Pendleton. Next to sentry duty at a Trump Hotel, being a Drill Instructor was still the best billet in the Corps. Roy's eight combat tours had earned his father the promotion and the plush duty station. Roy joined the Camp Pendleton group of Alcoholics Anonymous, shortly after the night in question, and he was sober now for two years. *Pretty soon pop might be a naked Digambara, like me*, Marty thought, as he opened the door and began to whisk his way across the portal. *Only it will be his insides that will be naked. This place is always squared away, but one never knows. According to the girls, Roy might have brought in some strange bedfellows.*

Monique was playing a video game, and she turned when he opened the door. "Marty! Where are your clothes? What's that in your hand? A broom?"

He made a whisking motion with his broom at her, his eyes drilling into hers in his best attack stare, as he covered his loins with his other hand. "Where's pops? I need to see him. You. Go to your room!"

She stood up. Her eyes were wide. "He's working out in the den. You're gonna let him see you like this? Are you freaking out or something? Is this for TikTok?" She grinned.

"Where's mom?" He shivered when the AC came on.

"Out shopping. They're having his graduated class over for a barbeque. Are you insane?"

"Get lost! I need to talk to dad."

Monique tossed the controller onto the couch and slowly dragged her feet across the wood floor toward her bedroom upstairs. Marty watched her climb the stairs, stomping on each step, and heard her close the door before he moved again.

***

His father was pounding the punching bag and doing jumping-jacks, which was his routine. Just as the Marine Corps had invented its combination of various martial arts and named it after themselves with the acronym MCMAP, Roy had invented his routine at home. He called this one PB&J for Punch Bag and Jumps. He had many more invented routines. It was his only form of creativity.

His father was six feet four inches tall and in superb physical shape. His chest was broad and tanned from running on the beach, and his two eagle, globe, and anchor tats—one on each bulging bicep--glowed with sweat from his workout. His buzz cut was graying at the crown of his forehead and on his bushy eyebrows. Marty could hear the air conditioner cut off, and the room became warm. He listened to his father's rapid punches and heavy breathing as he jumped, raising his arms in perfect coordinated rhythm and synchronization with the music of Guns and Roses playing over the fireplace mantle. Like most of the rooms in the house, it was very minimally furnished, which was the Marine Corps way.

Marty waited patiently, whisk broom at his side, readying his electronic hand for any activities that might ensue when his father first spotted him standing there. When he was drunk, Roy was a gutter mouth. When he was sober, he was a prudish Catholic schoolboy. Nudity was forbidden in his house, as was profanity, sexual innuendo, and any discussion of politics, other than the Marine Corps regulations.

When Roy turned toward him, Marty held his breath. *Here it comes*, he thought, and his hands clenched along with his jaw muscles.

Axl Rose sang, "I wanna watch you bleed!"

His father, however, burst out laughing.

"What the sam hill are you up to, boy? What kinda meds are those shrinks giving you? Is this your birthday suit surprise?" He laughed again, bending over and slapping his knees. "Okay, Martin, you've had your fun. Go get your clothes back on. You got me. What if Bernice and Monique see you like this? Jeeze Louise!"

"Master Sergeant Philips, I am reporting for duty. After I speak to you, I am flying to Madhya Pradesh in central India. I hope to become a Skyclad monk initiate. I want to become the exact opposite of you and everything you and your ethos and this country's ethos represent." Marty knew his father's mind would be blown at this point, and he was correct.

He saw the jugulars bulge in Roy's neck, and his face turned crimson. Not a good sign. "Skycaptain, what? Get your clothes on, Marine! That's an order!" his father shouted.

"I am sorry, Master Sergeant Roy Philips. I am no longer a member of the United States Marine Corps. I am a civilian, and as your biological progeny, and a legal member of this family, I am accusing you of the rape of one Jeanene Philips, whom you adopted, along with her sister, Barbara. On the night of October 12, 2019, while I was in Helmand, about to get my hand blown off from an IED explosion, you were in this house, drunk, screwing Jeanene, age nineteen. How do you respond, Master Sergeant? I have two witnesses. You have none."

In his entire memory, Marty could think of no moment when his father was vulnerable. Except for that moment. He watched Roy pick up a towel from the bench press, bring it to his forehead, and he wiped the sweat, just as the AC kicked on again. He sat down on the bench, looked up at Marty, and grinned.

"Hey, son. You know those girls. They were sneaking out at night to meet their friends. Smoking dope. Jeanene was the worst. She never talked. She just got stoned and sulked. Sure, I came home drunk, but I crashed. She came into my room. She wanted money. She's an adult. She's not my daughter. I told her she was a slut, so if she wanted my money, she needed to work for it. They both moved out the next day. I got off the booze, and now I've been sober for two years. It was a terrible mistake, I know. But she was a slut, Marty. You weren't here."

He stood a bit straighter in place, and he felt his scrotum lift his testicles into his body in fear. "Master Sergeant Philips, I am here to tell you that Barbara and Isabel are ready to testify in a court of law that you confronted Jeanene, Isabel, and Barbara that night with your Ka-Bar knife, and you kicked them out. You said if they said a word about what you had done you would get a platoon of your marines and hunt them down like Mazar-e-Sharif sluts."

Roy stood up. He looked around as if he were searching for that same Ka-Bar. "You've lost your mental faculties, Martin. All of those young ladies were unemployed drug addicts, living off me like leeches. I can get witnesses to testify to that. Their mother even knew. Jeanene and Barbara were just like their father. Criminals and drug dealers. You weren't here!"

Marty hesitated. It was true. He hadn't been around that year, so maybe things had gotten worse with the girls. But he knew the real answer, and he was ready to land his final punch to his father's heart. He pictured himself in India, following after his fellow monks, ready to learn how to carve the intricate and erotic designs on the temples climbing into the sky. Skyclad. Naked and proud of being non-violent. Proud of defending the defenseless. One meal a day. Worship at 3 AM. No lying. No stealing. No harming any living organism. The exact opposite of this man and this country.

"Jeanene just overdosed. Isabel and Barbara called me today while I was in my math class. Before she took her last heroin, she told my sisters what was going on between you and her. You were pimping her out to your jarheads at Pendleton, weren't you, Master Sergeant Philips? She got high, and they got their rocks off. Right? Isn't that the way it went down? You collected the money and gave her enough to stay addicted. Did you make money this way during your tours in-country? Huh? What about it, Master Sergeant?" He was shouting now, and he was crying.

Roy moved toward him. His face was contorted in rage. Marty's muscle memory kicked in. He knew his father could kill him with his bare hands, so he had to think fast. He had one more card to play.

"Did you know that in the Courts of California, a statement by a person on her deathbed is considered a fact which needs no other proof? Jeanene's confession to her sisters is admissible to a Grand Jury, and you, my father, my Master Sergeant hero, are as naked as I am. Except, your body is infested with maggots and worms, and every kind of squirming, disgusting creature that this world creates!"

With a great bellow, Roy Philips attacked his son, Martin Philips. Marty's electronic fingers, however, were robotic, and very powerful in their core design. They had to encircle very delicate objects, like a kitten's mewling face, or a woman's smiling one, but they could also grip steel balls and pull apart chickens for roasting, and so when they ripped into Master Sergeant Roy Philip's face, they did some terrible damage to his eyes.

As he watched his father's face bleed onto the wood floor panels, as he lay there, he recalled what Professor Huey had said about how the Hindu religion differed from Western religions. The West viewed existence in a very mechanized and orderly way, with a God out there somewhere, taking names and making divine and powerful judgments. This was how Marty had seen his accident on the road in Helmand Province. God on high had chosen him to be saved, and he should be thankful for being the only one out of the fifteen inside that APC to survive.

Now, however, as a Skyclad monk initiate, a Jain, he saw things quite differently. All of life was a drama, repeated endlessly, in which the heroes and villains pursued one another, and in this game of dramatic proportions, some could always remain heroes, and those who could always remain villains, and there were even those who could make their lives into living demonstrations to the world that one could exist without harming a single, living, breathing, and wondrous creature, from which all of Creation had sprung forth.

The airline tickets he had in his truck would have to wait until the trial was over, but he was still going to Kundalpur, even if he were judged a villain. Who knows? Perhaps one star-filled night, as he lay on his grass mat, staring up at the sky, nude to the universe and its follies, the Universal One might pour into him, releasing him forever from its ever-evolving karmic wheel of pain, pleasures, and sensory suffering of attachments? Perhaps in the stars somewhere, or on another plane of reality, there was a place where mothers, daughters, sons, and fathers were protected so well that they could love each other, every moment, forever and ever, amen.

The tears were filling his mask, but he did nothing. Even when Monique came into the room and started screaming, he stood stark naked and stark still. He pictured himself as the 57-foot statue that the Jains worshiped, the god Bahubali, which represented the first Jain to attain Omniscience. He became disgusted with living after having to go to war with his brothers. Every twelve years, the Jain disciples come to him to pour rivers of goat's milk, curd, and ghee over his head in celebration.

The Prophet

"If I had a God I could understand, I would no longer consider him God."—Meister Ekhart

I *am writing my first poem in Guatemala City. I do not go outside, as the gangs will taunt me, and the small gangsters will ride me, like a burro, whipping my ass with a tree branch, and singing some profane song. No. I am sitting beside the window inside the Orfanato Valle de Los Ángeles, run by the Franciscans from New York City. Our city streets have been overtaken by these hordes of drug dealers and pimps. I am fortunate to be hump-backed, Father Worthen, from New York City, tells me. The poem comes to me as it rains. Our little valley within the city is a bit rural. We have trees, birds, predator animals, and small prey. But when it rains, the children go out to play in the road, so I write an homage to them:*

> *There is no perfection. Only you. Sitting beside a window.*
> *It is raining. You can see the children playing in the puddles.*
> *They do not wait to see you, or anyone else.*
> *The paper boats still sail in the gutters like the giant tourist vessels going to other lands.*
> *The dolls are hugged tighter to chests.*
> *A dash of bravery, leaping up and above the strife.*
> *Coming down in the middle of the torrent.*
> *The tidal upheaval seems to pull your heartstrings.*
> *As the child flings the water, this way and that.*
> *And her laughter pierces your soul, for the moment, which is all there is.*
> *Suddenly, they all form a line, little soldiers with smiles on their faces.*
> *They dance, instead of march, and they come at you, and the streaks on your cheeks meld into the scene forever.*

I first talk to God the last time I am inside the chapel. It is the largest building at our orphanage. The photo we have on the

Internet shows the long rows of pews on either side. Down the middle leading to the small table as an altar, are the brown and white floor tiles, polished to a high sheen, and I can see my hunched-over body when I polish them with the electric buffer. Above the small altar, where the priest says mass, are the three giant paintings. On the left, Our Lady of Guadalupe, on the right, a Franciscan Priest, helping Jesus down from His Cross, and above, the Resurrected Jesus. I always think of the real God in this chapel, the clock above them all, with its golden spikes of radiance bursting outward, and the numbers in the center, controlling us all. 'MS-13.' 'Barrio-18.'

The voice of God tells me to pick up a Bible. I walk over to a pew and find a copy. I pick it up, its worn pebbled leather is comfortable in my hands. 'Turn to Luke, Chapter 17, verse 20 and 21.' I do this, and I read, 'The kingdom of God does not come with observation; nor will they say, 'See here!' or 'See there!' For indeed, the kingdom of God is within you.'

With nobody to explain it away, I take this into my heart. I vow to never open another Bible or read another book ever again. I will listen to God directly, as He is inside me as long as I can breathe.

What Anita has told me about the girl now makes more sense. Her parents were murdered by gang members when she was two, and she was given to the orphanage. Shortly after her chapel experience, Alicia was kidnapped by another group of Barrio-18 members, on her way to purchase food for the orphanage. She was found, a week later, stuffed inside the yellow balloon slide in the center of the orphanage compound. She had been raped, repeatedly, the doctor's report said, and she was naked, her hunched-over body slashed with knife wounds, especially on her hunchback. Some sadist had also carved a tattoo on the top of the mound between her shoulders. "Quasimoda." When Anita hired her to be a nanny for her infant child, Matilde, she did not speak one word.

As Meister Eckhart taught, becoming passive or silent was only an inward phase of reaching the God within. The Dominican was judged heretical in the Middle Ages because of his teachings. The same with Spinoza, who was excommunicated from Orthodox

Judaism. What did they believe? Nothing more profound than what the Advaita Vedanta believers in India taught for thousands of years: that God was either everything, or He was nothing. I am going to continue with the reading of Alicia's journal, as I am now wanting to discover just what she meant when she said she was going to listen to God directly. In my line of work, this was either a break in the mind, which then moves toward dissociative mental illness or the mystical life of the spirit.

"Anita! Could you please put on that Elgar album of the *Enigma Variations*? The one I use in my office when I talk to you? It calms us both, does it not? What I am about to read, I have a hunch, will not be very soothing. I want to quench the fire a bit with some quality music."

I can hear Anita scurry from the kitchen, where she was preparing her baby a milk repast from the mother's breast, which this mother keeps in the refrigerator to be heated. Soon, the strains of sweet ecstasy fill the room.

They spoke Spanish with their California accents, they wore no shirts, and their bodies were covered in dozens of tattoos, with the number 18 paramount, along with spiders, scorpions, skulls, dragons, and many scythes. These symbols completely covered their faces, throats, arms, legs, and torsos in weaving, black patterns. As they raped me, I kept hearing the voice of God, and I kept staring over at the standing boy beside the Pine tree. He had no tattoos. It was as if he were dropped down by God to protect my mind as it became twisted inside the sins being done to my body.

God said, 'Your body is but a shell. The true light of my power is within you. Focus, my daughter, on my inner glow. Focus. Look at him! He is my emissary. An angel to protect you. He will guide you on your path to reach the multitudes.'

I finally dropped into an unconscious state. As I did so, I had a strange vision. Hundreds of others, who were dying from the Coronavirus-19, appeared before my mind's eye. Each person wore a halo, such as I had seen many times in the books of my Franciscan teachers. A golden semi-circle and the face inside this halo was calm and reflective, with eyes looking up, mouth slightly open, and with no fear at all in the expression. Darkness came, and I awoke inside what I believed to be the belly of a yellow whale. God said, 'Do not speak. It is not time yet.'

It was Juan who saved me. The boy standing beneath the tree. Juan Chavez. He carried me back to the orphanage, and he followed me to San Diego. I did not know he did this until one day, as I was taking Matilde out for our stroll down La Jolla Shores Drive, he came up from behind me and almost caused me to flip the stroller in my fright. Up close, his eyes were green, and he was darkly handsome, with long lashes and a crooked smile. He was not a boy, as I had assumed during my ordeal. Instead, he was very slender and had boyish, innocent features. Black, wavy hair, a dimpled chin, and he did not appear to be put off by my hunchback. God spoke to me then, 'You may talk to him. He is here to help you reach out, and I will give you the words. I will also give you more if you are successful in reaching them.'

"Reaching them?" Was she becoming a messianic bipolar? It's quite possible. Combined with her parent's death and her rape at the hands of the same gangsters, she may have formed a reaction-formation to protect her mind.

It is now midnight. Juan has his smartphone set on a tripod holder, and I am seated on a chair in front of my desk in my bedroom. He tells me he will have many hundreds of languages translating my Spanish words. He climbs up the outside structure of this house very easy to get inside, as he used to harvest bananas before the corporate owners began using their robotic machines. I am a channel for His divine presence:

'Within the soul is a quiet chamber. It is where I dwell, your God and your Creator. If you will listen, as my daughter, Alicia, has listened, you will know the Truth. You must return to the Garden. Not to the Garden of Gethsemane, or even to the Garden of my Creative Paradise. Simply return to the garden of your daily universe. If you own no land to cultivate, then you must refuse to work at their factories, their businesses, and their other means of profit until they allow you to cultivate on their property. No land to cultivate, tell them, then no work from you. Resist, in the name of God! This is the first step toward Redemption. The second step toward Redemption is to stop killing any animal. You are all part of

my Creation, both human and animal, so why do you kill? Does it make any sense to you, those who have mental abilities to reason? Just because the people wrote about eating animals in the Bible? They are people. They are not Creators! They are blasphemers, not parents. The viral and other infections are connected to the greedy exploitation of the animal kingdoms all over this great Earth of mine. Your scientists have explained it, yet your leaders don't comprehend. I hear one of your scientists say the Chinese leaders can't shut the wet markets down because they are over 5,000 years old! How old am I? I am your Judge and your Creator. These Communists say they care about the land, and yet they torture animals and their people. They work them to death, steal the precious organs from out of prisoners' bodies. Use their technology to spy on everyone, just as you all spy on each other! Why do you spy? Why do you not trust? Because your ethos says to kill the first chance you get! Destruction and chaos are what you now believe. You would rather see division where there is unity. Fear where there is hope. Unless this all ends, this wanton greed and killing, then my reign on Earth will not take place!'

Juan tells me afterward that I am getting thousands of shares, and people are speaking in many tongues, making comments, seeing the truth in my words. He kisses me! I can feel the softness of his lips against my cheek, and tears come to my eyes. I have never been kissed by anyone other than by my parents or by the priests at the orphanage. My entire body warms with his touch, and I fall into bed. I watch him climb out of my window, into the starry night. This is only the beginning. The end is coming soon.

This explains all the crowds outside. She has begun a cult of followers. I go into the kitchen where Anita is holding Matilde in her arms, feeding her the breast milk in a glass bottle. "Why didn't you tell me she had formed a cult following?" I say, sitting down on a tall chair near the cutting board island.

"I know you wanted to help her, Anita. Your Catholic upbringing has been good for you in that. But now, Anita, I don't know what to say. This event has grown far beyond your assisting an immigrant. Has it not?" I am scrolling my finger on my cell phone, seeing the hundreds of articles about Alicia and her "channeling" of God. They are written by journalists from around the world. Both for and against her being a divine prophet. I am most interested, of course, in articles written by my colleagues. Here's one. Harvard Medical School. Head psychiatrist, Dr. Lance Bergman.

"Listen to this, Anita. Dr. Bergman says she is probably suffering from acute trauma caused by her rape and torture. I was thinking the same thing. This Savior Complex is rare, especially in women, but it is not without precedent. It can lead to acute psychosis, however, and even schizophrenia. What has she been saying lately in that room? Do you even know?"

Anita frowns. "I didn't want to tell you. I was afraid you wouldn't come over."

I move toward her, but then I remember the six feet distancing. I freeze. "That's not fair. What is it? Before I go into that room, I need to know!"

"Alicia has been instructing women. She says it's the last chance to save the Earth." Anita hugs her child closer to her breasts. Her business suit seems incongruous in this motherly pose.

"Instructing? I don't understand. How is she instructing them?"

"You've read the Greek play, *Lysistrata*? Spike Lee even did his version. The Spartan women decide to cut the men off from sex?" Anita half-smiles.

"Yes, of course. It was a comedy," I say.

"This is no comedy, Les. Alicia is teaching them how to orgasm without a man. Unless these men become pacifists, she tells them, they must no longer bed them. However, that's not all."

I wonder what more there can be. "Yes?"

"She tells them she can have sex with God, and that they can too." Anita shamefully hangs her head, like the little Catholic school girl she once was.

"Oh, Jesus!" I respond, meaning it. "This is worse than Jonestown or even Manson. She's beginning to condition these social media junkies into some kind of sex-bonding psychosis. There might be no limit to what they might do for her!"

She cries, and her baby starts crying. "Go in there at once, Les! She's having some kind of ecstatic fit or something. Juan told me he made love to her, and he orgasmed inside her, but she told him she couldn't climax with him. She pushed him off, and she stood up. She told him she was going to … I can't say it."

"Say *what*, Anita? I need to know before I go in there!" My heart is pounding in my chest and my temples.

"When the hateful comments came pouring in, and she saw that her words were being ignored, she decided to sacrifice herself. She is going to have an orgasm with God until she dies! She has a gun, Les. She is forcing Juan to film her … her suicide!"

All kinds of thoughts rush through my mind as I run toward that bedroom door. What can I say that might stop her? I don't know her. I don't even speak Spanish. I need to protect Juan. I'm not thinking of my safety, as all of this seems somehow pre-ordained. I have remained unmarried all my life for this moment, it seems. I can be shot to death by a grandiose and psychotic immigrant who believes I am preventing her from having the most stupendous moment in her nineteen years of existence. Alicia, a deformed young immigrant, speaks God's words, makes love with God, as Mary did before she had Jesus. To her, I am preventing another savior from coming into this world, and I might be the one sacrificed.

I am a tall woman. Five-eleven. But I am 74. I almost dislocate my shoulder shoving it against the bedroom door. Thankfully, it isn't locked.

The room is filled with radiant light. I can see her, sitting on the bed, her raven hair shiny with perspiration, her eyes looking upward toward the ceiling, in an obvious ecstatic pose. I remember seeing that same look in a painting by Michelangelo Merisi da Caravaggio I once saw at the Metropolitan Museum of Art in New York City. For some reason, the complete explanation of this painting appears in my mind's eye. It is not Mary, the mother of Jesus. Instead, it is Mary Magdalene, the whore Jesus forgave.

After Christ's death his faithful female disciple Mary of Magdala moved to southern France, where she lived as a hermit in a cave at Sainte-Baume near Aix-en-Provence. There she was transported seven times a day by angels into the presence of God, 'where she heard, with her bodily ears, the delightful harmonies of the celestial choirs.'

Alicia is not holding a gun on Juan. She is listening, and we all listen. It is the most beautifully rapturous music I have ever heard. Her blouse has fallen from her brown shoulders, and she tilts her head down. She is staring right at me. Alicia's amber eyes penetrate my being, and I can't move. We both do it at the same time, Juan and I. We fall to our knees in front of this woman. This disfigured young victim of violence, fear, and hatred. The hump that once made her Quasimota has disappeared! I can't help it. The tears begin to come, and I let them. I am no longer a scientist. I am just a woman. No. I am just a little girl. Playing outside in the rain with all the other boys and girls. We run toward the window, shouting in joyous abandon. The woman stares at us from inside, and she is beautiful! We all *know*. We are gazing at a miracle. I know I will protect this woman for the rest of my life.

The Church of Lady Haha

I am recording this for you all because it's an experience so trippy and psychedelic that it needs maximum exposure. I'll break it up into episodes so you can get the complete picture over our website. I'm not saying I am now a religious woman because of this one incident, but I am telling you that my attitude about living life has changed dramatically, and I just wanted to pass along the wisdom that I learned from one Fr. Barry McKenzie, S.J., the guy who came to me one day through my sister's web site, "Lady Haha's Exclusive Club," with our business motto "For Players Who Like to Play," in red, flashing 24-point Showcard Gothic bold font script, scrolling along the bottom of the page. I have made three thousand dollars an hour and fifty thousand dollars for a weekend, during my three years in the business, up until today. You see, being an exclusive call girl is like working on Wall Street or gambling in Las Vegas. You stay here only long enough to make your killing and then you retire. The dangers, however, are always out there.

Episode 1: The Gaga Connection

I've been with more men than I have even bothered to count, although my sister, she's Portia, says it's probably close to five hundred now, and that includes about fifty women who can pay the price for a date with "Lady Haha" or, as Portia calls me, "Little Minnie," because my real name is Minerva Louisa Puleo. She also says she's my "campaign manager" and not my pimp, madam, or quimp (queen-pimp). That's correct. My sister equates high-class prostitution with politics. When these rich potentates schtup you, they are mentally comparing you to all the other candidates in your party out there who are also lobbying to get what Gaga calls their special "vertical voting stick." Also, these rich bastards expect you to be intelligently literate and compassionate exclusively to their Madison Avenue, Wall Street Hedge Fund Manager, Chief Executive Officer, Governor, or Congressional tastes and lives. My sister's ability to screen our "players" is the secret to our success.

She has an M.B.A. from the Wharton School, and she sells real estate on the Upper East Side, where our folks live, so she is extremely business conscious, and she has personally made all the excellent contacts that are always necessary to the high-end market of the exclusive call girl business.

Also, since we both went to the exclusive prep school on Manhattan's Upper East Side, Convent of the Sacred Heart, the same school that the famous Lady Gaga attended, we have been using the fashions, music, and philosophy of the now-famous entertainer in our own business. However, whereas Lady Gaga attended the exclusive Tisch School of the Arts at N.Y.U., my sis and I attended New York high society's school of the cocktail party "touch." I kid you not. All of that Freddy Mercury and Madonna burlesque you see in those videos by Gaga? I have lived the real thing in classy hotel suites all across America.

Even though Gaga gets paid millions by her "korporate tykoons" to strut her stuff in computer videos and write songs for all her "little monsters," I have to finagle every deal directly from these corporate creeps using my imagination and my body—for real in real-time—and not on a phony stage or in an orchestrated video. They pay me extra for all my style and freaky sexuality, and Gaga is right about one thing in her philosophy. Most of these rich bastards just want to be entertained by eye candy: fashions right out of a porno flick--whale-bone corsets and fishnet stockings--complete with the googly-eyed, blond-headed-doll emptiness of a trained bimbo manga chick. They could care less about the emotional content of your act or whether or not you have intelligence that isn't related to them in some way. In other words, if you can dance freaky and look like a slut, then you're on the right track.

Truly. This is where Gaga and I part company in our respective businesses. Whereas she can show the final image of her gunnery boobs smoking, while her lover is on the bed beside her, his body fried like burnt lasagna, I have to suck that bastard's pimply dick or take it up the ass after my "real life" video. Portia and I have talked about this subject late into the night. The only person who can make another woman completely happy—both mentally and physically—is another woman. And, of course, this would piss the hell out of almost every guy who paid me, so it is kept a secret. It *was* a secret, I should say until Father Barry visited me.

Episode 2: Father Barry

Portia permitted Father Barry to visit me at the Regency Hotel on Park Avenue because he was the Principal of the Loyola School, the other major Catholic prep school on the Upper East Side. Besides, we both attend mass regularly, and we confidentially believed it was high time the Church allowed priests to get married and to even have a sex life. It would probably prevent all the sex abuse going on if the Catholic Church became more flexible about sex. However, as we discussed before Barry visited, the Church stopped priests from getting married in the middle of the first century because they wanted to keep all the money for themselves. If priests had their own families, then they would, of course, want to pass their inheritances on to their immediate families and not to the Holy Mother Church. Everything always comes down to money.

Portia gave Father the "cut-rate deal," which meant a Superior Suite, and not the usual Grand Luxury Suite, and he would not be getting the "Lady Haha Burlesque Routine" which was demonstrated online in the live video showing me doing one of my dance numbers almost entirely copied from one of Gaga's music videos. Portia said we were cleared legally because our school chum was now a world celebrity and what I do in my routine is, technically, a "parody" of her actions and not a direct copy of them. Anyway, it was a moot point, because Father Barry didn't want to watch me do anything of a sexual nature. As it turned out, all he wanted to do was talk and discuss what he called a "religious test" with me.

So, to set the stage for you, there I was, all dressed up in my best Catholic girl clothes, looking more like a Japanese schoolgirl in my uniform of *Evangelion* powder blue, pleated short skirt with straps, with a red satin bow under my white blouse's Peter Pan collar. The ruby slippers I wore were an excellent touch, I must admit. I thought this priest was probably thinking he was on a trip to Satanic Oz, so I would try to make him feel more comfortable playing Dorothy to his Wiz.

Of course, I was expecting some kind of voyeuristic trip, with him watching me strip down to Edenesque proportions, but was I ever surprised when he told me what he wanted us to do. First off, this thirty-something priest was somebody who could have honestly stepped out of the pages of *GQ Magazine*. His eyelashes were long and dark, and his licorice hair was spiked, and his torso showed a buffed and tanned man under his Hawaiian blue parrot shirt. His eyes were sea green, and the dimple in his chin made me think of that great character actor I love to watch in the old movies on TV, Robert Mitchum. He strutted into the room, confidently, and he sat right down on the chaise lounge, crossed his blue jean legs, and began stating his purpose for being there.

"Minerva, that means Goddess of Wisdom, did you know that? Minerva, I don't discuss my life before the Church with many people, but I do want to tell you that my mother was committed to an insane asylum back when they were called snake pits. She lost her sanity after my father ditched me and my sister and never paid us a cent of child support. I could tell my mother was insane because she asked me, just before she began existing inside her living nightmare, if I thought the world was eternal heaven or if it was an eternal hell? I suppose that was my first theologically big question, at nine years old, because when my sister and I became a nun and a priest, years later, after the Church had taken us in, I have been meditating on that one question for most of my life. My occupation before becoming the principal at the Loyola School was acting as the spiritual guide to hundreds of laypeople—both religious and non-religious—in month-long retreats at various locations around the world. These retreats consisted of my leading my flock through the entire 370 Spiritual Exercises of our founder, St. Ignatius Loyola. All members of the Society of Jesus must go through these steps upon entering, and these steps are the bedrock upon which our society reaches out into the world. After having led retreats in twenty-seven different nations, on eight continents, and in sixteen different languages, I have become quite an expert on these spiritual exercises. I am, most likely, as well versed in the world of spiritual cleansing as you are in the world of satisfying physical appetites, wouldn't you agree?"

I felt like I did in Catholic school. I didn't know whether the priest wanted an answer or not. They usually wanted you to just sit there and nod your head, obediently, but I suppose I couldn't stay quiet for a guy in a Hawaiian shirt. "Yes, I guess I know a few things about carnal pleasure," I told him, crossing my legs and looking out the window next to me. There were those same bustling cars and people down there, going about their appointed rounds, while I was up here talking philosophy with a priest. Only in America.

"Minerva, I have just read an essay that is forbidden by the Catholic Church, written by a man who was quite a literate fellow and who also wrote a futuristic novel you may be familiar with. It's called *Brave New World*. I suppose I read the novel in college, but I never paid him much mind until I came across this much smaller essay just recently. It was one of my students who gave me a copy, a woman you must know, and who has recently become quite famous in her own right. Her Christian name is Stefani Joanne Angelica Germanotta. She met me on one of the retreats I was conducting on the island of Corsica, in Spain. It was after she had completed the entire 370 spiritual exercises, and, I must admit, I was surprised when she showed up in my office. She is rather an intelligent young woman, and also quite beautiful, so when she laid this document on my desk I was quite receptive to its contents. What she told me, however, has brought me to your auspices for this religious test. She said, and I quote, 'Father McKenzie, you seem like a pretty nice guy. However, I think you need a retreat of a different nature. Read this essay and then see if you can get past all the verbal garbage for once in your life. Huxley says that the *Tibetan Book of the Dead* calls this experience seeing the clear light. What you now teach is a psychotic reaction to your mother's insanity. What this essay can teach you is to understand your mother's vision more clearly.' How did she know about my mother? Was she a psychic?"

As he paused, he looked at me with a questioning gentleness and sincerity. I was interested. "What's the name of the essay?" I asked.

"It's called 'The Doors of Perception.' In it, Huxley gives his personal experience taking a drug called mescaline, a cactus root by the name of peyote. It is used by the Native American Church, in their completely legal ceremonies, as a sacramental guide to witness that clear light. I want to take this sacrament with you."

I was dumbfounded. Not only was this priest breaking Church orthodoxy by coming to a call girl, but he was also now trying to take drugs with her! I must admit, I do eat a little weed in my Alice B. Toklas brownies and vegetarian spaghetti, but I kind of shy away from heavy drugs, and I didn't know what peyote was. "What's that? Is that like acid? I'm sorry, but I don't do shit that will mess up your chromosomes."

"No, it's a natural drug that reduces the sugar supply to your brain. Most mescaline users experience what's called the heavenly side of insanity. I think we could both use a little experience of this nature. I'm going to leave you this essay. Read it, and then get back to me. We need about eight hours together to experience this drug, and I'll pay you for the hours, no problem. It's just that my father was a big shot Wall Streeter who one day told my mother he wanted to get his sex from a girl who worked at her job as hard as he did at his trade. In other words, he left his family because he wanted to live his selfish life of professional manipulation, and he, in turn, was manipulated by women just like you. I just want to see if we can get past our egos and see what's out there for us—in a spiritual sense, that is."

Women like me? I would have stabbed a stiletto heel into anybody else's eye who spoke like that to me, but this priest's sad eyes told me a different story, as did his past. Maybe he did just want to experience a little hallucination from something besides his wine at mass and perhaps at dinner and in-between. I was up for the money, and I had a day clear the next week. "Sure, Father. Call my campaign manager. I can be here next Saturday, same time. Do you want me to wear anything special?"

93

"Read the essay. My purpose is to explore what my mother saw before she was locked up alone in her drugged state. The poet mentioned by Huxley, the one named William Blake? His visions were often seen as those of a madman. He saw the world through the seer's eyes his entire life. He wrote a poem called 'The Marriage of Heaven and Hell,' and these words will lead me to our rendezvous next week. Let me read them to you."

The priest took out a sheet of folded paper from his shirt pocket and held it up. "The ancient tradition that the world will be consumed in fire at the end of six thousand years is true, as I have heard from Hell. For the cherub with his flaming sword is hereby commanded to leave his guard at the tree of life, and when he does, the whole creation will be consumed and appear infinite and holy whereas it now appears finite & corrupt. This will come to pass by an improvement of sensual enjoyment. But first, the notion that man has a body distinct from his soul is to be expunged; this I shall do, by printing in the infernal method, by corrosives, which in Hell are salutary and medicinal, melting apparent surfaces away, and displaying the infinite which was hid. If the doors of perception were cleansed everything would appear to man as it is, infinite. For man has closed himself up, till he sees all things thro' narrow chinks of his cavern." He folded the paper back up and put it back into his pocket. "We need to open our doors, young lady, and I'll see you next Saturday," he smiled, and he left me alone to my thoughts.

Episode 3: The Drug Tryst

The week before my psychedelic rendezvous with Father McKenzie was typically energetic and routine. Most of the men I do are unimaginative, high testosterone types, who are into their bodies and not into their intellects very much, unless you count reading the *Wall Street Journal, Playboy,* or *GQ.* However, on the other hand, Portia and I were fascinated by the essay the priest gave me to read before our meeting. In it, Aldous Huxley, an author we had never read, gives you his personal experiences after ingesting the drug I was going to be taking, peyote, or the

94

psychoactive portion of it, mescaline. The coolest experience he described that I was looking forward to feeling was this "dissolution of the ego" that he described. In other words, the surrounding world became the center of attention and not the ideas in your head. For example, during that week, while I was dancing for these assholes, I kept thinking about what I was going to wear to my Saturday spiritual tryst. Simply because Father McKenzie did not care what I wore, it made me want to wear something completely special and appropriate. What I wore was especially important after we read the fact that the simplest things, like the texture and color of clothing and draperies, became imbued with fascinating and exquisitely mesmerizing detail. I decided I would wear one of my Lady Gaga knock-offs. Certainly, I would not be wearing the outfit of tied-together Kermit the Frog dolls or the plastic bubble dress. Huxley makes it clear that naturalness is key to this heightened awareness. Therefore, I decided to wear the red "catsuit" I saw in *Elle* that has red laced netting draped over your red thong underwear, with additional lace around your neck and on the forehead, with a portion that comes down in a spike just above and below your right eye like that guy from the old *Clockwork Orange* movie had. Since I already bleached my hair platinum, the blonde spiked hair that encircled my own, like a crescent halo from a Renaissance religious painting, would be a great touch. Meanwhile, these jokers in front of me had no clue. They were just taking in the eye candy, as I danced and flailed my chicken-wing arms in front of them, and they laughed uproariously as I shot off my Gaga pistol brassiere into the air like the Fourth of July.

Saturday finally arrived, and I was surprised to find Father McKenzie already inside the suite when I arrived. He was preparing the San Pedro cactus (*Echinopsis pachanoi)*, which he explained was a cousin of the Peyote but that it contained the same hallucinogenic alkaloids. He was cutting the long cactus, which had been stripped of its outer spines and skin, into naturally star-shaped slices, and then into quarters, and then tossing it into a frying pan along with some fresh onions and a half-clove of garlic. He then turned on the gas and began to stir, mixing in a half-teaspoon of salt. "This is called the 'Fried Delight,' because it takes out a lot of the noxious taste of this cactus. The San Pedro is not as noxious as Peyote buttons, but it can still stimulate your gag reflex," he laughed, tossing the mixture inside the pan over the gas flame of the range. Finally, he saw me, and he raised his eyebrows. He was again wearing a Hawaiian shirt—flowers this time--and jeans, but he was still very hot. "My, what have we got going here? You look like the cat that swallowed the canary. What's the occasion?"

"I just thought you might find me more sensually appealing when you come on to the drug," I said, and I wrinkled my nose at the bitter-smelling odor coming from the frying concoction on the stove. "Whew! Is this stink part of the test? It certainly doesn't send me into any Nirvana-like trance. It smells more like Nirvana the grunge group's underwear."

He laughed. "Go over to the home theater and push the play button. I chose an old video from the past for the occasion."

I walked over to the stereo system and pushed the button. The screen came alive with a black and white video from the early sixties. The lead singer, a guy that looked as hot as Father Barry, I might add, began to sing, "People are strange when you're a stranger. Faces look ugly when you're alone. Women seem wicked when you're unwanted. Streets are uneven when you're down."

"Hey! I've heard of these guys. Didn't their lead singer die in Paris?" I said, doing a little impromptu jig on the carpet.

"This group named themselves after that essay we both read by Aldous Huxley. They are The Doors. Jim Morrison was the lead singer. He was the son of an admiral, and he had an IQ of 149, but his love for America's drug of choice, alcohol, killed him at the young age of 27 in Paris. Huxley talks about how different drugs are banned by certain cultures. Why do you think our culture permits alcohol, tobacco, and soon, if the law changes, marijuana, and yet forbids drugs like mescaline?"

His question stumped me. I thought of drugs as being a social lubricant for those people who were too hung-up on religious morals to have any fun. "Hell, I don't know. I suppose if the government and corporations thought they could make money, then they would legalize it."

THE CHURCH OF LADY HAHA

"I don't think it's that easy. Remember that the drug we're taking is a sacrament that has been used by indigenous peoples for thousands of years. Unlike my Catholic religion, which is ethnocentrically based on teaching people to model their lives on their redeemer, the man-god, Jesus, whose teachings we, of course, gladly interpret for our parishioners, these native peoples, from what I've read, want you to see, alone, and for yourself, that God is everywhere around us, at all times, and that the problem with us is that we have purposely closed off our ability to perceive that infinite beauty and have replaced Nature's infinity with all the industrialized monuments to our self-obsessed glory. The drugs we legalize close the doors to perception. Alcohol dulls the senses and kills brain cells. Tobacco just plain kills you. Marijuana affects your memory and makes you over-eat, and, anti-depressants, if you're lucky, will simply keep your highs and lows from getting out of hand. Our current president is a perfect poster boy for our anti-depressant culture. America forbids us mescaline because it does not harm the intellect, and it gives one the viewpoint of the artistic soul. In other words, our leaders do not want a drug that destroys our ego because without our egos we cannot be manipulated through our senses. With mescaline, our senses become one with our universe, and our universe is seen in a clear light, and not, as the playwright, Ingmar Bergman called our post-industrial awareness of seeing life 'Through a Glass Darkly.' As William Blake would say, 'Our souls and bodies must become one with the universal. The Marriage of Heaven and Hell.'"

"Father, you're tripping me out. I never went to college, so I guess I'm missing a lot of what you just explained. It's like, yes, I want to see differently. My life right now is an obscene parody of Lady Gaga. She is the one with the inner vision that you describe. She's the artist. I guess I just rationalize it all to make myself feel better. You know, like the way you've been teaching the Spiritual Steps of St. Ignatius? I've been teaching the artistic visions of Lady Gaga. The Church of Gaga. We both have lost our unique vision. Maybe that's what we're searching for, you think?" I was surprising myself with this insight. Maybe just inhaling the cooking psychedelic cactus was making me introspective.

The Doors were finished playing, and Father Barry brought over the fried cactus and put the steaming bowl down on the glass coffee table in front of the chaise lounge. He also set down two tall drinks of lemonade. "You'll need to swig from this sour drink to counter the taste of the mescaline," he said, and he picked up his spoon and scooped up a glob of the light-green mixture in the bowl and held it in front of his face. "Eat up, and turn on!" he laughed, and he popped it into his mouth.

We both continued eating, alternating our digestion with drinks of lemonade until the bowls were empty. "It will come onto you slowly, so just relax," he said, so I leaned back on the lounge and closed my eyes.

It must have been about fifteen minutes when I began seeing things. With my eyes closed, I could see geometric shapes rising and falling, like they were on waves coming at me. These shapes were colored like a rainbow, and they also gave me a charge of energy. I opened my eyes and the room was a dazzling display of light and colorful objects that I had never really noticed before. It was as if the world had opened up its heart to me to explore her authentic insides, not the fabricated and man-made geometric shapes, but the soft-edged, creative patterns of something holy. Honestly, that's the only way I can describe it to you. Even when I looked over at Father Barry, who was sitting next to me on the end of the blue lounger, he seemed to be some object of art that was included in this wondrous painting I was participating in. Yes, "participate" is a much better word to describe what I saw than "observe" or "evaluate." I now understood what the priest had told me about losing your ego under the influence of this drug. The world in front of me was so interesting and full of passion that my wanting to judge it in any way or think about it was the furthest thing from my thoughts. Thoughts? How can I describe them? They seemed to also be part of the display, simple pictures that drifted in and out of the tapestry—playful things to momentarily notice and then let go, like one lets go of the handlebars on your bike when you're a kid, so you can feel the freedom and danger of riding without assistance from your metal propulsion system. Letting go. That's what it felt like. I was no longer in control of my world at all, and this new world didn't want me to think in those terms. I had to work up my courage to even speak to Father Barry.

"Are you seeing what I am seeing?" I asked, realizing just how inadequate words are and how obtrusive they are when you're experiencing a personal dialogue with the universe all around you.

"Yes, I believe so," he said, and his words seemed to float up into the air to me like music. I think I grabbed in the air at the streaming colors from the window that formed a pattern over our lounge, believing they were his words. Maybe they were! It was all so very possible in this new world.

"I'm going to have to write about this later," I said, looking down at the pattern on my red catsuit. The red seemed to bleed into my skin and envelop the skeleton of my leg. We, humans, wanted so much to change our bodies to attract notice. But, I realized, the "being noticed" was a reward in itself. Why should one cheapen the display with sex? If I am this beautiful and creative, then why do I have to give away my inner essence to them all?

Suddenly, Father Barry stood up and walked over to me. He seemed like he wasn't paying much attention to the objects in the room, the way I was. His eyes, which seemed somehow to be beacons that came from a different dimension, penetrated through my skull and out the back-side.

"What do you need?" I asked, intuiting that he wanted me to help him in some way. It was as if I saw the interconnectedness of all beings in this world, and he, of course, would always need me, as we all need each other.

"I'm living something again," he said, suddenly falling back over his legs and crashing down on the carpet. He looked up at me from his seated position like a little kid would look at his mother when he has crapped his pants. "I see what happened now," he said, and tears began streaming down his cheeks. "The door was closed all these years."

"What do you mean?" I asked, sitting down next to him on the floor and taking his hand in mine.

"I am at the bedroom door of my parents. I look inside and I see them. My father is trying to hug my mother and caress her breasts. She is striking out at him with her hands, slapping his face,

99

pounding her fists on his chest. He is asking her, 'Why, Beatrice? You never let me touch you. You reject me, and I can't take it anymore. I need someone to hold close and to love! I am only human, Beatrice. What are you?' I can see her face now, and it scares me. Her face is empty of emotion, the way it was when she asked me if life were eternal heaven or hell. She tells my father, 'You are all the devil's tricksters, aren't you? You just want to take my sacred flowers of the tabernacle! Well, you cannot have them. I won't give them to you. I am now Christ's bride! So, you can get the hell out!' she screamed at him at the top of her voice. 'Get out, or I'll cast you back into the fiery pits from whence you came!'

That was the only conversation we had over the eight hours we were high on mescaline. We did leave the suite at one point, and we each tripped out on the animals and people we saw as we walked along the busy streets of New York City's Park Avenue. Once we saw a woman walking her two poodles, and we laughed at her because we saw the same thing. She was being controlled by them and looked like a puppet on a string. However, when we saw a dog lift his leg to pee on a tree, Father Barry just nodded over at me and said, "He's praying." I could see the wisdom of his words in a deeply profound way. "You're so right," I told him, and we walked on down the road.

We finished up our drug tryst by watching all of Lady Gaga's music videos. Actually, "watched" is a bad descriptive word. That we "participated" in her display of cosmic humor, would be a much more accurate idea of what happened. Father Barry, at one point, took out a large book from his backpack and showed me the drawings of William Blake. We alternately viewed the drawings and then looked back on the TV screen at Gaga's dance video. One drawing especially provoked an inner reaction in me. It was called "The Whirlwind of Lovers," from Dante's *Inferno*. It seemed to encapsulate all that Lady Gaga was trying to communicate visually with her art. Blake showed us a twisting, living organism—like the bowels of some horrible bird of prey--filled with paired men and women--who were being forced through the fleshy whirlwind, naked and afraid, separated eternally from one another's caresses and embraces, and this was their punishment. I looked over at Father

Barry and I smiled. I knew how I was going to change my life, as surely as I knew he had had already changed his.

Episode 4: A New World

From that day on, I am no longer feeding the whirlwind of lovers. My sister and I have gone legitimate, and Father Barry McKenzie is helping us out. You see, what I realized was that selling my body, even if I were using the best STD protection available, and I was adding what I thought was entertainment to my act, I was still reaping the whirlwind of lust, so to speak, and I needed to change. If I didn't, I would probably get arrested and maybe end up like Father Barry's mother—a twisted, pathetic soul who had to escape her insane ego.

Today, I run what we call the "Church of Lady Haha." What does my "church" do? Well, we provide private retreats to anybody who wants to visit, at exclusive resorts, at classy hotels around the world, and at these retreats, we preach the marriage of heaven and hell. Father McKenzie no longer teaches the 370 Spiritual Exercises because he has resigned from his Catholic Jesuit Marine Corps commission and written his philosophical scriptures. He, too, wants to stop the whirlwind of lovers who are punished for being "merely" carnal and indiscriminate with their bodies. He wants to show all couples—gays, straights—yes, and even priests and nuns and other religionists who want their minds expanded, how to enjoy passionate and loving sexual play together, safely and without guilt. No longer are my sexual ratings and evaluations given out like some kind of fantasy football game.

Instead, I create my dance routines and my comedy about love and sex. For example, in one popular routine, I and my fellow actor, my sister Portia, wear stereotypical but exaggerated porno sex attire (ballooned out breasts, gigantic pink buttocks, and huge, fleshy, and fire engine red lips) and we begin a detailed discussion about what we like and don't like to have done to us in a sexually physical way. She'll pop one of my inflated boobs and say, "They are not there for you to win a Kewpie Doll! I want you to gently brush your lips, back and forth against them, until my nipples rise like the morning sun greets the day." Because I opened the doors of perception, I now have a new and legitimate career in the "sex business," and Father Barry McKenzie has a new flock of followers to tend. Yes, and since he is no longer a priest, he and I . . . well, we have opened up our communications to include what we have learned studying the world's best sex manuals, Masters and Johnson, the *Kama Sutra*, *Playboy,* and *Playgirl*, any book we can use to get ideas for our retreats. Our website is also quite awesome. We feature William Blake knock-offs because he inspired us to come together (Marriage of Heaven and Hell, don't you see!), and, as my sister Portia has pointed out, his works are now in the public domain. I guess since Barry has overcome his mother's hang-up, he has also become a better lover.

Religion? Glad you asked. We now belong to the Native American Church, as members in good standing, in Wilcox, Arizona. Despite the recent anti-immigration laws, Arizona usually respects the religious rights of our church, with its total membership of over 250,000. As laws evolved and court cases further molded peyote's legal position, the prospects for non-Native American peyote-based organizations arose. In Arizona, The Peyote Way Church of God and The Peyote Foundation can operate because the exemption from prosecution is based on religious sincerity, not on race, denomination, or physical boundaries. Oregon has a similar statute with the exception that it is specifically not applicable to the residents of correctional facilities.

Four other states have slightly more stringent requirements. Peyotists in Nevada, New Mexico, Colorado, and Minnesota must be members of a bona fide religious organization, including the N.A.C. or the American Indian Church. Some states' statutes could legally permit a non-Native American to sit at a peyote meeting if it were run by the N.A.C. Others require actual N.A.C. membership, some even of Native Americans. Unfortunately, Texas, the native habitat of the peyote cactus, has the strictest requirements for exemption from prosecution. Texas exceeds the federal guidelines by requiring that a person be not only a member of the N.A.C. but of at least 25% Native American descent.

THE CHURCH OF LADY HAHA

Peyote's religious exemptions do not ensure freedom from prosecution as the burden of proof still rests with the defendant. Evidence of spiritual practice is often called for in a court of law. Even in Arizona, where the exemption has been upheld and is well known, we are still subject to persecution due to the over-handed and unconstitutional scrutiny applied by the War on Drugs. Father McKenzie and I find it quite distressful that our country still wishes to condemn drugs that are thousands of years old and that facilitate the insightful experience and make our connection with Nature more enjoyable and yet we still must protect ourselves daily from the government.

The Visionary

My mother called me "genius." She said I saw things that other people did not see, and what I expressed was from a place deep within the Mind of Jesus. My mother said Jesus had changed into somebody much different when He was a twelve-year-old Jewish boy, and I had also changed. She explained that when Jesus was finally tortured, crucified, and buried, His Mind never disappeared. Instead, it was sent out from his holy corpse to become fractured by the sun and shattered into billions of tiny shards of light. These holy shards were sent throughout the universe and penetrated the newborn heads of children chosen to have genius visions the way I have them.

I have accepted my fate. Other children have ridiculed me and teased me because of my visions, even my two older brothers. My one twin sister, Guadalupe, who protected me, was to become a sacrifice to the Mara Salvatrucha, or MS-13. They were targeting young girls to make money from their young bodies in our village of Sonsanate. I tried to explain to them how they were acting, unlike the tribal warriors they were impersonating. They were imposters, I said, and I told them when the ancient tribes took someone's life in battle, they would always return to the enemy tribe's home to make amends for the lost soul and pay tribute to the lost warrior's family by giving them some food or other tribute. I tried to explain that my sister needed to determine her destiny as this was what freedom was. We are Ladino, I told them, so we speak Judeo-Spanish, and our heritage is closer to Sephardic Jews than to Catholics. We are mestizo or Indian, so we are outcasts in that respect as well. Our tribes always gave back what they took away, in equal measure, I told them. The modern world does not recognize true freedom, I said because thought is always selfishly dividing everything into categories, geometric shapes, and lines of demarcation, the same way you have drawn lines on your bodies. The modern world has created so-called invisible "laws" that keep a barrio of control around us so we cannot have our freedoms at any time.

The leader of the MS-13 was a tall and skinny man with tattoos resembling skulls, scorpions, and scythes. These symbols completely covered his face, throat, arms, legs, and torso in weaving, black patterns. He placed his hand on my forehead and tipped my rather large head up to meet his black eyes, and he told me I was a very wise child. Someday, he told me, I would become a leader like he was, and then I could have my freedom. In the interim (I was surprised he knew this word), he needed to take Guadalupe to pay for our family's insurance.

When I asked about why we needed to pay this insurance, he said some of his *compadres* were going to take us north to freedom. To do that he needed insurance in the way of my sister's young body. She was twelve, and her chest buds were flowering that year. Wasn't our escape to freedom a form of tribute to our family in the way of the ancient tribes? He asked me. I did not answer him. He then laughed, and I could see that his teeth had many gold fillings. He told us we would have to send money each month back to him to pay for our continued freedom. Or else, he said, and he placed his right forefinger beneath his chin, at his throat, and swiped it across. He also pointed to a skull on his chest, and we all knew what he meant.

Mother and father were crying, and my two older brothers told the gangsters they would do anything to keep Lupe from going with them. Finally, the leader agreed, and the eight other members beat up my brothers for thirteen seconds each and initiated them into the gang. Ramon and Carlos were scratched all over their bodies and sniffling blood from their noses. But we were going to be led by two gang members by train up north to Mexico and on to the Texas border near Brownsville. My brothers would stay to cook meth for the MS-13 to earn our passage to freedom.

As we rode on top of the crowded freight train, I kept telling our coyote escort gang members that I had been struck by a sliver from the Mind of Jesus, and whatever I said would come to pass, just as our Lord and Savior was able to predict His future. As I saw they were smoking cigarettes of marijuana and laughing, I knew they would never believe me. To them, I was just some humorous curiosity on our trip north. That's when I had the first of my three visions. I call it my "Vision of the Father." As my words were shouted into the noise of the day on top of the swaying box car, I kept seeing the two gang members' black eyes becoming wider and wider.

"This is how the Father created all of this. He was alone in the Garden, one day, as the sun was about to rise, and He decided He wanted to be entertained. So, from out of His Mind came a most beautiful woman, and He called Her the Mother of Humanity. She was so beautiful that He could never take His eyes from Her. She was, in her wisdom, a Creator in Her own right. However, whereas the Father created the matter out of which all of our creations have been grown, this Mother of Humanity went all around this new world and made it beautiful by etching the fine details we all love to enjoy. She also made music to accompany this new wonderland. As She danced from flower to flower, watching them blossom for the first time, the Father's eyes followed Her. She then began to create the animals, the insects, the rivers, the trees, and the mountains, giving each uniqueness and beauty all their own. Something wondrous was happening as She did this. The Father had to move His head so quickly to keep up with Her activities that he began to pop out new heads to be able to watch Her from every direction on the landscape of creation. When She finally began to mold the bodies of the humans from out of the earth, His many heads exploded from the miraculous sight. These small humans were so like Him that He was instantly struck with pity. She had created the most wondrous creatures imaginable. Each being had within him or her a piece of the exploded heads of the Father, and he or she also had been crafted by the most beautiful and loving Mother in the universe. They were, however, forever to be cursed by the fact that the Father's jealousy gave them free choice, and this would place them forever in fear for their own lives because of the complexity of the endless choices available. These humans did not want to disappear from the loving, musical, and peaceful comfort of their new Mother and Her home, yet they had to go forth to travel their way to make the choices necessary to please this ever-jealous and ever-watchful Father, who was now buried deep within each of their bodies, like an eternal tombstone of Fate."

The two gangsters breathed out their marijuana smoke and stared at me for several minutes. They finally looked back at my mother, father, and Guadalupe and told them I was *muy loco*, as crazy as a demon child on the Day of the Dead. They said my name would now be "crazy demon," or *demonio loco*. However, they took turns sleeping on those starry nights, as we made our snake-like way toward Mexico. One of them always kept his eyes riveted upon me as if he thought I would curse them or place them under a hypnotic trance of some kind. I just smiled, ate the tortillas and cheese my mother gave me, and slept, waiting for my next vision.

***

When we arrived in Mexico, we were taken by rental truck over to the Rio Grande, where we would cross by boat from Hidalgo into Brownsville, Texas, our destination. Our gang escorts held knives to the throat of a boat owner in Hidalgo and told him to take us across. If he did not, then one of the MS-13 members in Mexico would pay him a visit when he was least expecting it. He, of course, agreed, and he was told there would be no problem with border patrol agents because the gang members were going to call in to report a small boat crossing the river twelve miles from where we would be crossing. When the agents traveled upriver to stop the suspicious craft from crossing, we would be safe crossing down here.

I had my second vision, which I call the "Vision of the Son," as we were crossing the Rio Grande by boat. I told it to my family and to the boat's owner, whose name was Eduardo. I thought I would stand at the bow of the boat, the way I had seen pictures of Jesus doing when He was on the Sea of Galilee. I looked out toward the Promised Land, the U.S.A., and I spoke into the misty, parting waves below me:

"The Son of the Father was created one day when it was decided that humans needed some kind of advocate for them. Like the Mother, the Son was created out of the Father's Mind, in a dream-like state. The humans believed the Son to be one of them, as He had the same physical form, but He came at midnight into their midst, and He was never born. He was already an adult male. The humans had already begun dividing things with their thoughtful,

107

greedy minds. Thus, many languages were spoken, many beliefs were adhered to, to pay tribute to the high priests, gurus, and other so-called spiritual leaders. In the same way, many other leaders formed cabals of political governments to oversee and distribute the land and wealth that was all around them. Even though they could have shared everything equally, very easily, without shedding one drop of blood, it was their simple minds that made them desire more than the next person, and it was their simple minds that fashioned selfish measurement and value on different objects and people, to make the world a conflicted, complex, and war-torn place. The Son saw all of this, and He knew that true intelligence was not thinking with the mind, but seeing and experiencing with the mind, body, and heart as one. This was the way it was before the Father had His dream, and so it was when the Son was born into His dream. Each of us, He explained to them, comes to dream his or her desires, and we try to make the dream real. We never stop to see that it is this selfish dreaming that keeps all of the worlds apart. The humans nodded their heads, as they could hear some truth in what the Son was telling them, but they secretly whispered behind His back that what He was saying was blasphemous. Each human secretly believed there had to be unlimited freedom to acquire as much wealth and protection as he or she could reap before almighty death took him or her into its vice-like grip. Sharing equally and living peacefully were impossible and quite out of the question. Therefore, since the Son was one of them, and was made mortal inside the Father's dream, the humans rose against this wandering minister and took him on a boat out onto the river to be drowned. However, just as they were about to grab onto Him and thrust His body into the waves, He began to dance. He was channeling the energy from His Mother, the creator of beauty and music, and as He lifted his left leg and crossed it over His right leg, He pointed down, and beneath His perfectly balanced right leg was the figure of one of the humans from the village, the high priest. His poor, stunted body was being held down by the Son's leg, so He could dance. One of the humans was so transfixed by the music coming from nowhere, and by the rhythmic undulations of the young Son, he began to thrum upon a small drum he wore around his neck on a strap, as a good luck talisman, whenever he ventured out upon the boat. As he thrummed the human beat of passion, at one with the joy and the dance of Life, the lightning began to strike from dark clouds, which had formed above and all around the boat. Just as one of the humans tried to dance along with the Son, he or she was struck down by a bolt of lightning, and he or she was transformed into a black, smoking cinder. When there was only the dancing Son and the pilot of the boat left, the dark clouds began to recede, and the pilot was alone, quivering in fear. The pilot asked the Son if it was over. As the Son continued His dance, He looked down at the pilot and smiled. Death is never over. Life is never over. We come, and we go. Death and Life are the thrumming heartbeats of the universal Love of the Father. It never ends. After He said this, the black cinders suddenly took their human shapes again, and the re-born humans who were inside the boat followed this Son until His dying day, and His teachings were spoken to others throughout the generations of humans to be born. The thrumming of Life and Death was a gift to them all, and the dance of the Son was pictured forever, in the dreams of humanity."

***

My third and final vision came after our little family became separated. We first became part of a huge crowd of people entering Brownsville's processing center for crossing the border illegally. This is what the translator woman told us as she was helping us fill in the forms required of us. When my mother explained that her two sons were being held in El Salvador to pay for our trip into the United States, the woman asked who was holding them and for what reason. She told her that the Mara Salvatrucha came to our home and was going to take Guadalupe. Mother pointed to her daughter. But then, when I, Felipe, told them a vision I had about the early tribes in El Salvador, they said they would accept her two sons instead. In return, we would get a free escort to where we are today.

The woman told mother that we could not obtain asylum if we were running away from gang violence and that the President's order required that we be separated and placed into different holding quarters. Mother and father would go to federal prison, and Lupe and I would go to different facilities in Brownsville. Mother began to cry, asking her if there were any possible ways we could stay together. She said that I was a special boy, a genius, and our entire family did not mix well with others from our country because we were Ladino. Mother asked if being Ladino were an exception to gain asylum, but the woman shook her head sadly, no. She told us we would all be together in a few weeks, and then we could go back to where we came from. We could not stay here because we were not being given legal asylum. My mother began to scream at the woman that if we couldn't pay the gangsters in El Salvador, they would first kill her two sons, Ramon and Carlos, and then, if we made it back to El Salvador, they would kill us.

The woman said she was very sorry, but there was nothing she could do at this point, as it was the law given by Executive Order, and she pointed to a wall poster showing the image of the President of the United States. I noticed he was smiling, with a healthy fluff of golden-blond hair and a blazing red necktie. He looked like somebody's rich uncle. Just like Uncle Sam.

My stay at the Casa Padre was uneventful, even nice. We were over a thousand boys then, housed inside what they said was an old Walmart warehouse. They fed us regularly, we had video games and computer school, and the beds were five to a room. To be honest, it was much better than our home back in El Salvador. I simply had to wait each day, as the days turned into more days, and then my mother would call on one of the many telephones around the warehouse to tell me where I could meet her, Lupe, and father for our trip back to El Salvador. I kept thinking, even dreaming, about what I would do to save my family.

The gang leader said I could be a leader one day, so I wondered how this was going to happen. When one of the hundreds of workers would call for us to get into bed, I knew my fate would be much different than the boys around me. They had all told me that they were getting asylum because they had been child soldiers or they had relatives who could sponsor them in the United States. I was the only one who was going back. At least, it seemed that way to me.

***

When we returned to our village of Sonsanate, we were still together, and my father and mother said that was what was important. I was not so certain, as I knew we had to face the same gang that had sent us away and who wanted Lupe. However, I had thought a long time about what I was going to tell the leader, and I was prepared.

He sat in a wicker chair in the center of our house, reading the newspaper from San Salvador. To the right and left of him stood my older brothers, Ramon and Carlos. Now, they too had the many tribal tattoos decorating their bare-chested bodies. We did not hug or kiss. It was not acceptable to their new machismo code of violence. Near the back of our single-room house stood a short boy, of about fourteen, who was from the rival gang called Barrio-18. I could tell, as he had a large eight-ball tattooed in the center of his chest among the other tattoos, but instead of figure eight, it had the numeral eighteen.

The leader finally looked up from his paper. He smiled.

"Greetings, travelers, he told us. I heard you were not warmly accepted into the land of freedom. I was just reading about their president, Trump. He has called us animals to be destroyed, and we are so horrible that his country will not take anybody who is, in any way, associated with us. Funny thing. He does accept his rich gangster friends from Russia who can afford to stay at his fancy hotels. They have their children there, it says, and they immediately become United States citizens! And he has the gall to tell poor Central Americans that we go to his country to have what he calls 'anchor babies.'"

I asked him what his name was. He had never told us.

He smiled again.

"My name is Smiley. Your name is Crazy Demon. Her name," and he pointed to Guadalupe, "will be Crazy Chick."

111

I now understood their code of logic. By remaining anonymous, they could circumvent the laws and stay in the shadows. But what was going to happen to that poor boy standing in the corner with the rag in his mouth wrapped with tape?

"Crazy Demon, you now must become one of us to save your family. If you do what I tell you, I will allow your sister to live and work to keep your parents alive in the village."

Smiley pulled a small pistol from the pocket of his baggy slacks and spun the cartridge cylinder. He told me to shoot this bastard in the head, and he pointed toward the rival gang member. If I did not, he told me, he would have Curly, and he motioned to one of his henchmen standing nearby, shoot Crazy Chick in the head. Curly took a gun from his pocket and moved over to hold the gun at Lupe's head.

All I could think about was the vision I was having about life and death. As I took the gun from Smiley, I began to orate what I was dreaming, walking calmly over to where the rival gang member was shaking and crying. It was my third and final vision.

"When the Father realized that His dream had become insane, and there was no way out, except to gradually make it destroy itself, He sent a ghost into the dream where the humans lived. This ghost could enter any of the human bodies that existed, and once inside, it took on the personality and life of this human, male or female. However, since the entire dream had to gradually turn into a destructive nightmare, so it could dissolve and become reborn into the Garden Paradise before the Father's dream, this ghost turned humans into monsters. These monsters were selfish, greedy murderers, who never saw the good in anyone who was not like them or who did not fit within the strict guidelines of law and order as they understood them. The Father was secretly the ghost. He was incognito. There was a method to His madness, as it was, of course, only a dream, and it had cycles of good and evil, creation and destruction, wealth and poverty, and on and on. Without these opposite and eventually destructive forces, there could be no entertainment for the Gods. The greatest entertainment of all was how the Father could become incognito to inhabit any one of His creatures. These monsters were fulfilling His plan just as the saints in the dream fulfilled His plan. However, when it came time for death, the humans had the last laugh."

I was standing next to the young gang member, and I held my pistol up to his temple, about to send a projectile into his imprisoned mind. I could hear his whimpers in the shadows, and I could smell his sweat.

"For, you see, these humans could also have dreams, and theirs were just as powerful as those of the Fathers, Mothers, and Sons from the eternal realm. All of humanity and all the dream world were one, and the dreams of the humans were, therefore, the dreams of individual Gods as well. And thus, all was correct inside the flow of the infinite cycles of expanding and contracting cosmic justice, inside the universe of Fathers, Mothers, Sons, Daughters, and incognito Ghosts."

I turned around quickly, fired once at Curly, once at Smiley, and I pointed my pistol, hot and smoking, at my two older brothers. My dream was now real, for the moment, and we were, once more, a family.

Asterisk

A Corporate College in the United States of America, 2045.

I t is a calm, breezy day outside. Inside Room 15B-12, my friend and mentor, Dr. Hal Bernstein, is talking to me, one of the few English professors on campus.

"Look, Ralph, you won't even know they'll have them. The robotic surgery leaves no scar, no blemish, or trace of any kind. The kid will look just like the rest of them—without the zits--except, of course ..."

"Except they'll know every fucking answer before I will," I interrupted my old pal from the Computer and Social Science Division, Dr. Harold Bernstein. It was degrading enough that we professors in the Humanities and Literature Division had to have a personal "guide" to explain new tech to us. Now we couldn't even have a say about which students had technological advantages inside our classroom.

"Look. It's like this. These kids will soon be entering our classes, en masse, whether we like it or not, old buddy. *They* are the chosen ones. It ain't my people. You remember what happened when we tried fighting the system back in '17 when they got rid of Net Neutrality. They spun it all by telling everybody it would be a better method to individualize instruction, work, and entertainment. That's been computerization's gig all along. They called it the *5G Revolution* back then, remember? Kurzweil's Singularity and the evolution past the problems of biology. You gotta go with the flow. Think of it this way. Either they plug into their phones or they get an implant. The old public Internet we grew up with is long gone, my friend. Democracy was a fraud, anyway. We knew it was all about the competition. Beneath all the Socratic and hemlock-eating bullshit. So, just embrace the future!" Bernstein wrapped his short hairy arm around my broad shoulders.

I've been an outdoors and exercise fanatic all my life, and Hal has always been the prototypical techie—slumping shoulders, diminished frame, and poor eyesight. His idea of exercise is coding a new application for Masturbation Fantasy, the popular Wi-Fi gaming community.

We are both eternal bachelors, at 58, and getting ready to cash in our retirement chips, but we agree on some things, like our taste in android women and our love of computerized baseball. Football? Forget about it. It's all robots now. No head injuries but boring as hell. And the last vestiges of the old-fashioned "American Pastime" disappeared back in 2020 when AI was inserted in all the players, and "android enhancements" were allowed to be used by those clubs who could afford them. They worked these enhancements into the sport the same way they used to negotiate for players who had special biological talents—like a 100-mph fastball. The quadrillionaire owners bid for them, and the competition stayed the same, but the players could now play longer and perform better. Hal and I were doubtful ourselves until we saw our first 700-foot homerun hit inside a ballpark. The fences, of course, have extended a lot since that historic moment, as you might expect, but the fun's still in the game. At least, I think it is.

"So, how about it? You can tell who they are by the asterisk beside their names. You know, the way we used to tell veterans before our combat military became all-android and remote-controlled. Now the human vets and active-duty personnel are all top-secret developers. These new AI kids are the same way. Top secret. The plutocrats' kids. We used to have to give them all A's, but now we don't need to put up a front. Remember how you used to protest grade inflation? Then I figured out how we could defuse the chip implants, and we took them out to party in the city."

I chuckled. "Do I? Those rich little bastards looked at me like they owned me. I told them I was giving them two grades. The grade the Administration forced me to give them and the grade they earned."

"Right. And where did that get you? Nowhere. Those rich kids still went on to inherit their family's businesses, or they sat inside some executive office whacking-off, for all I know. Today, there's no need to hide anything except by giving them an asterisk on the roster. We don't even have to challenge it anymore.

Remember old Jesse Jackson, when computers first came into play?" Hal nudged me in the ribs with a fat index finger. "Huh?"

We said it together, "You gotta be a guide on the side and not a sage on the stage!" We laughed.

I let out a long sigh of resignation. "All right. I'll just let them cheat their way through. It's like you said. It makes no difference now anyway. I just want my retirement. I want to live in some nuke-safe bunker and read classic literature, until the assholes blow us up, or destroy the planet with their mechanized and computerized pollutants."

"That's my optimistic colleague! Don't rock the boat. I'll see you at lunch tomorrow. We can go to the new Android Sex Palace tomorrow night. It's all clean, all-satisfying … and," he waited for me.

"All sexy!" We both said.

As I watched Hal walk away, I felt a headache beginning to develop in the back of my head, on the right side. I took a few steps to leave my computerized classroom, and I became dizzy. I steadied myself with my arm against the door. The dizziness finally passed, and I looked into the iris recognition viewer and the electric door slid open, and I stepped out into the quad.

The sun was going down, and it was its usual gloomy self. Smog-laden clouds were strung out along the horizon like a heroin addict's dream, and the setting sun looked like a gray-orange, stainless steel ball falling amongst the eucalyptus and palms—which were genetically defended from the pollution, the way we humans were soon going to become. After this AI experiment, we would all, most likely, lose our humanity forever.

After all, I thought, as my head began to throb again, *why do we need our flesh and blood bodies? This current brand of evolution has only one ultimate destination if we are to survive at all. We have to become non-human, all-android, and proud of it! Unless, of course, I can stop this so-called progress.*

I held my head between my palms as I walked toward my self-driving compact car in the teacher's underground parking lot. *I need to convince these kids that what they'll be getting into is not worth what they'll have to become. They must be still young enough*

116

to listen to reason. Hell, the Communist Revolution began with the wealthy kids, didn't it? Why can't I be their Marx and Engels—their Chairman Mao and Uncle Ho? I'll show them what it's like now and what it will inevitably become tomorrow if they keep playing Pluto's game.

***

The next afternoon, after I had done my mile jog around the track, my class appeared, and I looked down at the roster. As I scanned the names on the tablet with my finger, I noted the asterisk beside the ones who had their AI implants. *Waverly, Wanda June; *Sebastian, Earl Wendall; *Wang, Jill; and *Peters, Alan Steven.* I needed to figure a method to get them to stay after class without raising any suspicions. We were going to be doing a dramatic reading of Flannery O'Connor's short story, "Everything That Rises Must Converge." Two of the few topics permitted in college literature classes were ethnic diversity and sexual identity. These were very positive, in the estimation of the Administration, as long as these kids realized their social lives were always under the constant surveillance of the corporate authorities. Mixing races, mixing genders, and equalizing everybody down to a colorless and throbbing pulp, was what this new society was all about. As long as the students never criticized the overall plan of control, it was quite proper to discuss how we must learn to live in harmonious joy. The pain was beginning to throb in the back of my head again. I grabbed it with my right hand and massaged it.

"Class, after we have selected the people who will read the different characters in O'Connor's story, I will go over the message of the piece and what this great writer was trying to say. To explain further how the parts are to be read, I want the following students to stay after class today so I can further explain what their parts will be exemplifying. Ms. Waverly, you will play Mrs. Chestny, the bigot. Mr. Sebastian will play her son, Julian. Ms. Wang will play the colored lady on the bus, and Mr. Peters will play his little boy. The rest of you will play the minor parts described in the story."

I then told them to pull up the story on their tablets. I gave them my usual summary of how O'Connor was a Catholic, by religion, and that she often used Catholic themes to weave around her story and her characters. "For example, what do you believe the title of this story relates to, symbolically?" I gritted my teeth to try to stem the pounding of my headache along the ridge of my forehead.

As suspected, the four hands of my AI implants went up immediately. "Yes, Ms. Waverly?" I pointed to the blonde-haired and blue-eyed girl of 17 or 18 sitting in the front row. She wore the usual harlot-in-waiting outfit these girls all seemed to perfect; fishnet stockings, garter straps, short skirt, push-up bra, and tattoos that could be seen along the arms and up the neck (in this instance, a dragon spewing flames under her chin); all taking place beneath a blouse that was see-through and chintzy. With all the money these kids had, one would imagine they could affect a more refined decor, but no matter.

Ms. Waverly stood up and pronounced her answer in calm and, no doubt, perfectly copied verbiage from her implanted intelligence within: "The quote comes from the French Jesuit Priest and idealist philosopher, Pierre Teilhard de Chardin, in his essay on *The Future of Man*. He is discussing whether atheists and Christian believers can, because of their similar faith in the positive future of mankind, reach the same destination. Followed to their conclusion, the two paths must certainly end by coming together, he says, for like things, everything that is faith must rise, and everything that rises must converge."

"Very good," I say, knowing full well she was replicating a direct quote from the memory of the giant database stored in the corporate computer and sent out by Wi-Fi signals to her brain. "But does that make O'Connor's story title realistic or perhaps ironic?"

Blank stares from the entire class. If I had perhaps been more direct as to my specific reference in the story, or as to a character or a scene, my four implants might have come up with something. However, as I knew, a computer cannot compute analogous or metaphorical thought. Therefore, in this isolated instance, I was still more powerful.

"It is completely ironic in terms of what happens in Miss O'Connor's story. The bigoted mother, Mrs. Chestny, and, to a certain extent, even her college-educated son, Julian, believe that the Southern Negro can never rise equally with whites—either on Earth or in Heaven. And thus, it goes against this Catholic Jesuit's teachings. Of course, you will all see this more clearly when we read the text on Friday." My head pounded, but I managed a smile. "So, you may all go home and read the story, and those four of you I named, please stay back for a few moments if you would."

All four of my implants remained, as instructed. I stood in front of them, rubbing my temples, as the headache was now in the front and back, throbbing uncontrollably. I had the sudden urge to become impassioned and influentially doctrinaire, something that was quite forbidden in all my 30 years of teaching at the college level.

"Your parents control the means of progress in this country of ours, do they not?" I asked, knowing my rhetoric might confuse their implants.

Earl Wendall Sebastian, the Julian of our story, spoke. He was biogenetically perfected, like all of this spawn of the wealthy, but his clothes, again, were torn jeans and what appeared to be pajama tops. "Yes, our parents provide the society with the intelligent means to become systematically improved, day by day, in an orderly method of calculated perfection."

I reached out and performed a forbidden act. I touched the Peters lad on his shoulder blade. He pulled back instantly, his face grimacing. "Why did you do that?"

"Have you ever seen or touched anybody of the underclasses in this society of your parents' making?" My voice was low and threatening as if I could scare them into reason.

"No, of course not. It is against the law to mix with them except in isolated and protected settings, such as this. In school."

"Yes," my head throbbed, "and only you and I know this unwritten law, do we not?" I was moving into hazardous territory that could get me arrested and perhaps even flown off to a terrorist torture camp in Syria, Afghanistan, or other such secret prisons of the corporate authorities.

"Quite true, Mr. Sentry," said Jill Wang, a dark-haired, pig-tailed lass of about 16. "The workers are important to our objectives, but they can never achieve the status of their leaders." Ms. Wang's parents were probably from the elite in the Communist Party, who were always purchasing companies and properties by the thousands, and who sent their children to school in the United States just to prove to the wealthy back home that they were internationally progressive.

"Yes, I understand. But did you know, Ms. Wang, that Communism once meant that all property was to be owned and maintained by only the workers? You and your parents are not Communists, anymore, at all. If anything, you are greedy, usurping Capitalists who have hijacked the Communist religion for your purposes!" I got the words out, but my head was so painful I had to drop it down between my knees, as I sat back upon the desk in front of them.

I could feel their eyes boring into the back of my head. *What should I do now? The moment had to be seized.* I stood up and stared right back at them, my eyes red from the intense pain of my torturous headache. "Come with me. I will show you what you've been missing."

***

A s we walked out to the demarcation zone beyond the campus walls, I understood the seriousness of my actions at last. What I was now doing meant an immediate suspension and termination, as well as arrest for violation of the Federal Corporate Ordinance that I signed on the day I became a teacher. My job was to teach the "theoretical knowledge of symbolic art and literature, and to never reflect upon the reality of the societies known as the underclasses, which were off the Wi-Fi grid, and not in the purview of the elite leaders of corporate America." The minute I broke this law, I was subject to arrest and imprisonment. I was no longer a teacher. I was, in fact, a terrorist.

I knew these students traveled to and from the campus in tunnels built to enclose and shelter their self-driving vehicles, keeping them in the dark from the reality existing outside all around them. They journeyed from their protected, gated community to the school, and never once did these implants and future leaders ever touch any of the others on campus, who came from the workers' city beyond the campus walls, and they certainly never touched one of the teachers.

As I extended both of my long arms around their shoulders—Sebastian and Wang on one side, and Waverly and Peters on the other—I could feel their bodies tense up as if they had been electrocuted. This was why we could never touch. When we did so, we defused the implanted chips in our arms, and we could walk freely past our confines without being monitored. When we slipped past the ivy-covered walls, we could hear the flying drone guardians whining in the inky night, and I began to feel them relax.

Outside the campus, in the workers' city, we walked, arm-in-arm, taking in the sights, smells, and sounds of the evening. If one person from the administration or faculty happened to be slumming it, I would be reported. Thankfully, we saw nobody I knew, and as we walked into a nightclub, my implants began to pay attention. These underclasses dressed the way they did, for one thing, but theirs was the clothing of poverty and necessity, collected and sewn on ancient machines from decades past, and pieced together reverently, and without any commercial fanfare, as none of these underlings were allowed to view the entertainment airwaves of the chosen elites.

These workers spent most of their days doing all the jobs necessary to maintain the highly affluent and secret lifestyles behind the walled and gated communities beyond—like the colleges and the skyscrapers--the hermetically sealed and genetically isolated realm of the corporate power-brokers.

We walked into the non-technological entertainment den of these flatlanders—these trash sifters and electronic garbage haulers—these uneducated, yet very human workers, who labored for survival, scrounging for their reward, for the daily cast-off vegetables and meat replacement protein goop, raised inside the laboratories and the gardens of the synthetic and unnatural farms, hidden deep within the corporate farming zones throughout the city.

Their lives were brief, brutal, and without much joy. And yet, as we walked amongst them, we heard their rhythmic, speech music, watched their passionate dancing—something between the jazz-age rebelliousness and wartime jitterbugs of bygone years—and we became filled with something that was never present in our protected zones. We felt what it was like to experience actual freedom.

My students began to study the young and old dancers—something that was never permitted in their habitats—the mixing of the young and the old—and they began to dance with them. As I watched their youthful bodies, off the grid of the Wi-Fi, my headache began to slowly recede. I could smell the foul odors of marijuana and a crude alcoholic brew made from some kind of fruit, and I took one of the drinks handed to me by a smiling maiden, and I sipped it deeply, and I smiled, perhaps for the first time in my career as a teacher, and I thought about the connection I would teach my students tomorrow.

The convergence of humanity must take place in the real world—not the virtual one—and if we can realize the common goal of future survival as a species, we can begin to branch together, forming a tall tree of brotherhood and sisterhood, sharing the fruits and the labors—not just for the elite few, but for the majority of our brothers and sisters beyond the wire. Their corporate parents were attempting to completely affix their brains into the digital empire of nothingness. Virtual reality was never real, and they now knew they must rebel or become blinded forever.

When the sirens began to wail, I did not care. My implants stood beside me, their asterisks were meaningless, and their jaws were clenched tightly, as their youthful arms encircled my tall body like tendrils growing straight out of the Catholic and Atheist Garden of Eden itself. *Everything that rises must converge*, I thought to myself, as they hauled me away into the dark.

***

The first voice I heard was Bernstein's. It was the same, high-pitched, New York accent. As I opened my eyes, I could see him standing beside my bed. The room was lit with early morning light, and I could see it was an infirmary of some kind because it had the collection of monitoring and computerized gadgets I saw each year when I received my physical exam, inoculations, and the newest genetic enhancements.

"Ralphie! You're still alive, all right. The Doc told me you might be, but I didn't believe him until those lovely blue peepers of yours popped open. How do you feel, old pal?" Bernstein combed his pudgy fingers through his curly-black, implanted hair. It was his only claim to masculine physical enhancement, as he wanted nothing to do with human women. The feminist backlash had ruined our love for what used to be normal relationships, and we had embraced our android lust and Stepford Slut lifestyles with gusto. We had figured if the corporate entities now controlled population growth, anyway, then why should we be controlled as the "perfect consumer family" that was monitored at all times and kept from experiencing the wild lifestyle that only singles could live?

"Did they arrest me? What about my implant students? They were defending me out in the workers' city. It was beautiful, Hal. I think they finally understand why we all need to pull together to make things great again."

Bernstein stepped over to me and took my hand. He never touched me. The concern on his face scared me. "What are you talking about, pal? Don't you know why you're here?"

"Yes, I tried to teach my students about how the underclasses live outside campus. They were dancing in a club, and then the sirens began. They stood around me, holding me and protecting me. That's all I remember until this moment."

"No. That's not what happened. You assaulted one of those students, Ralph. Alan Peters. You know you can't touch a Pluto kid. But the doc told me why you behaved so badly. It's not your fault." Bernstein squeezed my hand, and a few tears dropped from the corners of his brown eyes. "You have a brain tumor. It was pushing against your implant, and I suppose you weren't thinking straight. He says he can get the robots in to surgically remove the cyst."

"Brain tumor!" I remembered my headaches. "You mean, we weren't outside campus? The students didn't try to protect me?"

"The pressure on your brain must have caused you to hallucinate, pal. But you'll be back to normal after the surgery, I promise. Except for one thing." Bernstein hesitated.

"What's that? Did I lose my job?" I could think only about my future.

"No, not exactly. However, until the corporates see you've come back to us, you'll be flagged on all the drones and cameras." Bernstein frowned.

"Flagged? What do you mean?" I bit down hard on my lower lip. I could feel the pain, and I liked it.

"They're giving you an asterisk beside your identification hologram. Until they're certain your brain problem has been remedied." He saw that I was not soothed, so he continued. I didn't hear his words, as I was thinking about getting out of bed to run, to exercise, to fill my body with endorphins to soothe my existential agony.

"The implant kids liked your lecture about O'Connor's story. They did! You just can't touch them. We'll go out to the Sex Palace right after you've had that tumor removed. I promise. They have a new model of seductress. Donahue was telling me about her. She can do anything … she even knows baseball … all the players, their current stats …"

I closed my eyes and pictured the tumor inside my head. Soon, I knew, there would be no tumors, no biological problems at all. Just the mechanized perfection of a new society. The Singularity. I sighed deeply, but I knew, ultimately, it was for the best.

Valley of the Dogs

To get you into the atmosphere of what my life is like, I'll take you to a scene earlier in the day it all went down. As dogs know best, shit does roll downhill. And we dogs are at the bottom of that hill. It was an Ash Wednesday morning, and me and my cohorts, Koji and "Miss" Asia (she's the alpha female around these here parts) were getting our ashes from Cowboy. He's a born-again, New Age Catholic, so we have to suffer for it. He even has this giant red cross painted on a rocket ship fuselage hanging up in his room! Asia, of course, is his pride and joy. Because gays must have a thing about female dogs or something. Can you tell I have a bone to pick with fancy-ass bitches? Both of them—human and canine.

Asia sleeps with Lady HaHa, or GaGa, or Raja (never can get human names straight) at night, while Koji and me get stuck with the Cowboy. I call him Cowboy because he wears that dumb Howdy Doody hat and his outfits are color-coordinated by John Wayne Gacy's Pogo the Clown alter ego. Get my drift, buck-o? Our humans are certified whack jobs.

Funny thing. More of us dogs are learning the talking gig every day. Who wouldn't learn to talk, with all of your podcasts blasting out all over the place? CNN at the airports, media everywhere; in your toilets, in the shower stalls, up your asses, if you could get enjoyment out of it. Dogs and cats will be running things down toward the end of times. You wait.

Miss Asia and Koji are mute as stones. As deaf to my world of angst as a dog biscuit or a Cowboy's hat. Or, one of GaGa's steak dresses. Anyway, how long's it been since you've been in the wild, dude? The *real* wild, not back-packing or celebrity hiking. Our species has always had one foot in the wild, even when you dress us up like you do. I'm the only one in this family who can speak and think in educated language, in real, philosophical words.

Back to Miss Asia. The star of this freak show, our wealthy owner LaLa, gives Asia, the prima donna, her own Instagram page. And she holds Asia in her arms on the cover of *Elle* or *Bazaar*. Her small, black, and shined-up body gets greased for the cameras. They even dilate her adorable pupils with drops of Belladonna. She was the first French bulldog bought by YaHa, and Asia told us she used to get baked with our owner back when she got lit up on ganja like a Christmas goose, while she wrote those first hit songs. "Bad Romance" and "Alejandro," which she wrote the first year she bought me.

After that re-make movie about the drunken Cowboy singer, Miss RaRa said she wouldn't get high anymore. Good. She already lets Asia sleep on her Fendi Peek-a-Boo bag, wearing a pearl necklace. Me and Koji, on the other hand, are lucky if we get ten minutes of rack time on the Cowboy's treadmill, or he lets us watch Earthquake Calhoun wrestle on the oldie's computer station. We also got our balls whacked off. Cowboy got that duty. I'll say this for him, he can cry at the drop of a hat. Never see many humanoids do that, especially male ones. But he does. Cried over *us* getting *our* balls whacked off, just because our masters can't respect free sex in nature.

***

D Don't get me started about Asia.

Okay, so you get too much time on your hands when you're owned or employed by a multi-grammy-winning artist, full of money, who has about as much common sense as a soggy dog biscuit. And you're stuck in lock-down with them during a pandemic. You listen, as she explains to you, waiting to go inside the studio in Hollyweird, to record her albums, and she talks about how "dogs are smarter than people," and then I begin to think that she's coming to her senses. Naw! Because she turns around and buys Ass-kiss a new diamond collar and yoga pants, and we two boys get bupkis. What a life. These two humanoids. They're either crying about how everything sucks, or jumping around and dancing like maniacs. I've never seen these humanoids do anything dog-daring, like sprint after a kid on a bicycle, or chase down a neighbor's cat.

Did I already tell you about the Cowboy's room, especially on the day it all happened? As I said, it was Ash Wednesday, and Cowboy was telling us about how we all—humans and dogs—have to die and that it was all right because we're immediately turned into stardust. Shot right back up there into space, I guess. Now that's not how dogs think about heavy shit like that. We believe our Poet Laureate, Allen Ginsberg, and his masterpiece, and our theme song, "Howl." Now here is some *real* philosophy: "What peaches and what penumbras! Whole families shopping at night! Aisles full of husbands! Wives in the avocados, babies in the tomatoes! --and you, Garcia Lorca, what were you doing down by the watermelons?" Not during this lockdown. No way, Jose. Nobody's shopping like that, Allen. We're stuck with GaGa and Cowboy and Thai food home delivery. I hate Thai.

Are you laughing yet? In that humanoid way, you all have, with only two ways of finding humor? One way is any expulsion of air from any of your orifices, which immediately sends you into a laughing frenzy. If we do it, in front of you, it's even funnier! If you take a video of us, and we fart, it goes viral in fifty seconds, upon "Valley of the Dogs," and you send it as a video file to Neil Patrick Harris. The second way humanoids find humor is from the inventions of your super-creative brains, like LaLa's music videos. When she shoots guns out of her boobs or wears steaks on her body. We rather enjoy that one. Here's a suggestion from our dog poet laureate, Ginsberg: You don't have to waste your creative powers on music videos or dog fart sounds. No, you just chill out, listen to your favorite music, and snuggle with your favorite mammal. Us.

***

That's what I was thinking about on Ash Wednesday, as Cowboy was getting his New Age rocks off with his philosophically meager insights about humanoid and dog life, existing in peaceful coexistence and shooting to the stars when we die. Thank Dog, when he finally finished marking a cross on our foreheads with his organic curry powder, and we got our dumb-ass organic doggie health food treats.

Here's another fact about dogs you may not have learned. We have the world's worst case of ADHD. Attention Deficit Hyperactive Disorder. Do you know? The point, sniff, run, fetch and repeat? So, these obsessions we have cause us to constantly be aware of things. Mindfulness? We invented it. We are so distracted by living in the now that we're like the dog version of your Beatniks. We're like that dude in Poe's story, *Berenice*, that Cowboy read to us one time. We get focused on one thing, like your stupid grins when you watch us doing anything, and we stare back at you, waiting for food, but it never comes, and you still keep smiling at us. And it becomes an obsession with us until we finally want to pull all your stupid, smiling white teeth out. Slowly. With pliers. One by one. But we can't. Because we've got paws. One of your brilliant merchandisers even named a brand of our food after our "paws" disability. What if we named your food "Brains," which is your disability?

Cowboy's room? Did I describe it yet? Lots of pinks. Pink throw pillows. Pink throw rugs. Posters of pink ballet dancer humanoids. But then there's a puke green chair shaped like a humanoid's colon. And posters of the Hollywood Gay Pride Parade. It's like living in Dante's Seventh Circle of fashion Hell. But it is home, of sorts. But not like GaGa's room. Her room is a boudoir of celebration to gayness and nature. When you're in there, man, you don't know whether to take a leak on a hibiscus, eat a baby palm, or dance to YMCA.

And then, that Ash Wednesday, after we got our ashes and treats, it was that time when every canine and humanoid in the world joins together in bliss. Cowboy was so stoked about the experience the first time that he named the Instagram page he put up for us "Valley of the Dogs." Cowboy's kind of artistry. Let me explain. *Valley of the Dolls* was a pulpy, popular book and romance movie about rich women like YoYo and gays like Cowboy, who stay plastered all the time on psychoactive humanoid pep pills, blow your mind pills, slow your mind pills, or shut down your mind pills (both temporary and final shutdowns). Cowboy and YaYa, Asia told us, used to get high together A LOT. That was their favorite book. That was their mantra. After they both got clean together, just before she bought me and Koji, they decided it would be "cute" to put up this Internet page and name it after their favorite novel about drugs in Hollyweird.

Dogs never need that stuff. Know why? I told you. Our ADHD. We're either out like a light dreaming about trees, running, and getting our testicles back for a few fantasies, or we're wide awake like a snake in the bottom of Death Valley, except we're dogs, so our paws get hot easy. Cowboy once took a picture of me. The only one he ever took that was arty. I am laying on the cracked ground, in Death Valley, because Cowboy thought it was cool that the Manson Family once lived there, and I looked in his photo like a desert dog dying in the sun like a humanoid. Like a dog version of *Treasure of the Sierra Madre*. On my back, my hind legs crossed in a crooked way, my tongue lolling out of the side of my smashed-in face.

Do you know why we learn tricks from you? We think it's funny as hell. You want us to be so far into your heart we can both see Paradise, but because we can learn to speak (bark), or roll over, you're supposed to be the master? Ha! We know when we do those stupid tricks of yours that we get closer to you. Hell. You love us. You spend more money on us than any animal in the world. Get a clue, North American humanoid. I watch National Geographic. They eat dogs in China, South Korea, the Philippines, Thailand, Laos, Vietnam, Cambodia, and the region of Nagaland in India. I saw the graph on Cowboy's computer. Yin and Yang. It's dog eats dog or man eats dog. We enjoy the good life, partner, I know, but if you get that dog-eating glow in your eyes one day. Let's just say two can play at that game. Read any *Cujo* lately? Koji's got his Cujo act down pat right now. Watch-out! Woof!

I know, you're all thinking we're nothing but three little Frenchies, from a powder-puff humanoid country, France. No French fries. Freedom fries! So, we're supposed to be powder-puff dogs, and we can all live together in this family like wimpy fruitcakes. Look carefully. Really. Don't we look like they took a frying pan to our mugs and poured greasepaint all over us? We aren't over thirty pounds, soaking wet. But we've got you trained.

***

Here's the part of my story that gets scary. Trigger alert! I need to get into my Stephen King Zone. That's the part of the subconscious that's been trolled by the Shadow until it puts the entire world into a horrible, existential bubble. A novel virus, anyone? The competition between the humanoids and the rest of us mammals. Humanoids want everything so fast, and so much of it, that our living quarters are getting beaten down. When the water and air are no good, the future is not so bright. That's what it was like that night. That Ash Wednesday morning was a portent of the horror to come.

Our reward was that Cowboy was taking all three of us for a walk. That's as if a humanoid who's into kinky sex gets to have three of any kind of other humanoids he or she wants. We French say *menage et trois*. Three neutered dogs get to go out. Happy Days are here again. Get those masks off my face! Get that cute sweater off my back! I'm rolling in the grass, peeing on trees, barking to heaven, and sniffing any asshole I can find in my vicinity. Do you ever get that kind of satisfaction, humanoids? Why do you take so many pictures of us? Dress us up in clothes that my wolf and coyote brethren do stand-up dog comedy about. Did you see Gustav and Koji wearing those darling candy cane sweaters with the words "My tongue, your face," or "Your dog doesn't know sit," etched at the top? Aren't they adorable! Such great examples of the superior canine species. Can you give us credit for having a brain?

All right. We're out the door with Cowboy. He has his blue shorts on with the pink belt, and his blue shirt and green pea soup tie, with the Peewee Herman rainbow jacket. I think he was yammering to us all about how we're going to fly with LaLa out to Italy for the movie she has to shoot. Telling us how lucky we were to be living with people who love them so much, kissy-kissy, and who do so much for them. Yadda, yadda, yadda. Same humanoid exaggeration.

Slow down your pace a little bit, gay blade, we gotta go pee here! Cowboy always wants to run, so he can show all the other gay blades in the neighborhood how fit and tight-butted he is. Sheesh! You can't even sniff them! Butts. All we wanted to do that night was study the starlight and take in the scenery. That night I was forced to speak. Out loud. For the first time. These things happen, right? It's very humanoid. He finally stopped and pointed up to the stars. He got into his stardust preaching again, and we were supposed to be mesmerized, I suppose, but I felt like it was time to tell him what was lacking in the humanoid world. So, I told him, right then and there, on the sidewalk next to the public thoroughfare:

"Cowboy, you and the humanoids have to do something about your greed. You take too much, and you forget where it all came from. You forget the animals and the humanoids in your so-called deprived countries. We dogs, and most of us animals, do only those actions that give back to our natural world more than we take out of it. Not a big deal. Take a leak, the tree thanks you. Wag our tails, you guys go crazy. If you'd pay attention to what we do once in a while, maybe you could learn something. I blame this pandemic for this breakthrough. When we get forced to have a time out and live closer to you, to be more intimate, so to speak, we need to *talk* to each other. We dogs live in a constant crisis because of you. Not just a climate crisis. A crisis of values."

The white rolling thing came out of the fog, its eyes shining directly ahead. We were passing in front of our house, and we knew she was watching us from the second floor, pushing back the lace curtains and smiling out at us the way she always did, and Cowboy was singing "Over the Rainbow," or some other fruity song because I guess I had freaked him out with my speech. He was probably thinking about all the money he was going to get by putting me out on tour with GaGa. At least I could upstage Asia for once. I can't sing yet, but I can do the howl bit when she sings "Bad Romance."

I was thinking about all of this when two of *them* opened the back door to the white car, and they had black masks on their faces. They both, of course, went after the larger males, that's me and Koji, and left the bitch, Miss Asia. Males are worth more on the black market. Do you know about those times when there's a noise that can scare the turds out of both dogs and humanoids? Although truth be told, we trick you into learning how to take us hunting with you, because we know what a wagging tail does to your brains. Listen. It's just scuttlebutt I heard from my colleagues visiting from the hunting places in our country. Needless to say, our Cowboy was no hunter. He was a Midnight Cowboy. He was a hunter for love, maybe, but nobody had to worry about getting Ninja'd or American Snipered by him. So, he does what he does every time a spider is on the wall, or Asia throws up, or LaLa gets angry with him. Or she wins another Grammy. Or I talk to him for the first time. He screams.

He began slapping back at those two assailants. He went total dog on them. We protect our own, and that's what Cowboy was doing. When they grabbed me by the collar and hauled me away, Cowboy let out the first piercing scream. I mean, the scream he reserves for when Neil Patrick Harris visits LaLa backstage. Then, when they got hold of Koji, Cowboy went berserk. He spat, screamed, scratched, slapped, and pulled at the one guy's arms. Then, as I watched from the back seat, the one being assaulted by Cowboy pulled what looked like a dark dog biscuit out of his pocket. I thought maybe he was trying to teach Cowboy how to sit up or rollover. No. I heard the second most horrible sound you can ever hear. Unless humans can train us to avoid it, this sound will keep us hunkering down in the weeds. Fourth of July? Forget about it. It takes *you*, my humanoid friend, to pull us up and to get us to trail your prey, or to fetch your bird or a bigger animal after you make this sound with your metal dog biscuit. Do you want to be the master? This is what makes you think you are. But when I saw Cowboy lying in his pool of blood, shot four times, it was time to remember what Cowboy said about the stars and how we're made of the same dust.

And, then, as the shooter got into the white rolling thing, carrying me, I could see he was crying, too. He took his mask down, and he was just a young humanoid, shivering with fright like I do whenever Cowboy yells at me. I knew this was the time to speak again. These boys will have to lie some more, cheat some more, steal some more until they get put inside one of those concrete tombs

Cowboy shows us on his computer. He told us, "We house more humans in prison than any country on Earth," and his eyes squirted that liquid humanoids have ready to spray, just the way we can piss on a tree, or against a table leg, just the way we can whine for our walks, or cry for our food, or just the way we can wait for you to come home. You take us into your warm arms, nuzzle us with your faces, and smother our bodies with your kisses. Do you think we don't want to talk when you do that? That's love, man. That's *real* love.

And Cowboy taught us all about all the wars, and the bombs, and the shootings on the screen. We watched all of it with him. Not until that Wednesday night did it make any sense to me. I was too filled with my world to understand him. He said they were out here in the world. He told us we were better, and we believed him. We whined, and we ate his food, and we listened to him because he was speaking from his heart, not his brain. We can understand when that happens. It happens to us, also, and that's when you say we smile. When we can understand, we get to reach another level. That's where I was on that Ash Wednesday night. Another level of understanding.

That's the moment my Stephen King Zone changed into my awareness zone. I had become humanly aware. You were no longer humanoids to me. You were very human and very dog. Even this other human, the one who had just kidnapped me. So, I spoke to him:

"You left a dying man back there. And we're three dogs who will never see him again. He taught us to believe in the stars and feel the light of life. I never really saw that light before now. We are made of the same stuff, and you need to see it also."

I was finished with my first sentence when they both turned toward me, sitting next to my life's pal, Koji, and they both began to bawl. Like frightened babies. The one with the gun talked to the other one. "Did you hear that? Did you want to do that meth? You suck, man!" Mr. Yin, up there in the driver's seat. Mr. Yang, back here with us. They whined so long and hard that when they finally made it out of our neighborhood, they turned right onto Hollywood Boulevard and took us to another house nearby. It was an old female human's house because she came running out, as fast as an old human can run. One by one, each of her human children took us up into his arms and carried us out to the old lady. Their eyes looked the same way Cowboy's eyes looked after he was shot. I saw Cowboy's face, even in the dark, because I was standing at his feet. We dogs get used to looking up at you all the time. We see a lot, and we feel a lot. Believe me. These two young human men had heard me, and more importantly, they had heard their hearts.

They raced away with their white rolling thing, into the rest of that night, and we both looked up at the remaining human. The old female and mother. We thought the only natural and obvious event had taken place. She was teaching her young ones to fetch. We now knew about how they were killed, but we still didn't understand how they lived.

When she picked us up, we didn't know what to do next. She walked us the six blocks back to GaGa's house. She even let us pee. She didn't know about the reward then. She didn't know about how Cowboy had survived the shooting, four shots passing through his body, not a single one hitting a vital organ. The cops, and the news reporters, and the tears of GaGa as she took all three of us into her arms. I didn't have the heart to tell her. I could never speak again.

When Cowboy got out of the hospital, he never heard me speak again. He told himself it was just part of that magical Ash Wednesday night. He was in shock. He was a trauma victim. Dogs don't talk. Miracles might happen, but dogs don't talk.

Until we do. When you need it.

ABOUT THE AUTHOR

James Musgrave's work has been featured in *Best New Writing 2011*, Eric Hoffer Book Awards, Hopewell Press, Titusville, N.J. He was semi-finalist in the Black River Chapbook Competition, Fall, 2012. He was also in a Bram Stoker Award Finalist volume of horror fiction, *Beneath the Surface, 13 Shocking Tales of Terror*, Shroud Publishing, San Francisco, CA. His historical mystery series starring Detective Patrick James O'Malley was selected as "featured titles" by the American Library Association's Self-E Program for Independent Authors. The first mystery in that series, *Forevermore*, won the First-Place blue ribbon for Best Historical Mystery, in the Chanticleer International Clue Book Awards, 2013. James lives in San Diego, and is the publisher of EMRE Publishing, LLC.

Sign-up for the Author's Newsletter at emrepublishing.com

www.ingramcontent.com/pod-product-compliance
Lightning Source LLC
Chambersburg PA
CBHW072028170626
46811CB00008B/2980